Renegayd

David Kraine

Copyright Kraine Kreative 2018.

Cover Illustration: Daniel Conway
Cover Design: JAKE!
Chapter Illustrations: Elwira Pawlikowska
Formatting by Polgarus Studio

Print: 978-0-9898108-4-5
Ebook: 978-0-9898108-5-2

Burst down those closet doors once and for all, and stand up and start to fight.

— Harvey Milk

Contents

Foreword vii

The Scales of Justice 1
Chapter 14: Love Crimes 3
Chapter 1: Spin Spin Spin 7
Chapter 15: Making Lemonade 21
Chapter 2: The Queen of Witches 30
Chapter 16: Out of the Closet 40
Chapter 3: The Spectrum 51
Chapter 17: Global Rights Organization 62
Chapter 4: Enyo 69
Chapter 18: Echoing Cavern 79

The Ivory Tower 89
Chapter 5: Love's Detour 91
Chapter 6: Orgiastic Flute Melodies 105
Chapter 7: Forging the Scales 113
Chapter 8: Sugar and Cinnamon 120
Chapter 9: Healing 134
Chapter 10: Utility Positive 144
Chapter 11: Monochromatic 151
Chapter 12: The News Cycle 159
Chapter 13: Picking Sides 164

The End of the Rainbow 169
Chapter 19: Resistance 171
Chapter 20: The Third Way 178
Chapter 21: Transister 184
Chapter 22: Progress 200
Chapter 23: Fruits of Recruitment 209
Chapter 24: The Birth of Tragedy 217
Chapter 25: Blank Canvas 230

Foreword

What if every action has an equal and opposite reaction?
What if LGBT advancement is equal parts erosion?
What if each organization fighting for equality has one pushing back?
What if light on a disco ball creates as much shadow as sparkle?

Let's imagine the fight for LGBT equality is a game of football. (How's that for the beginning of a book on gay rights? Don't worry. The glitter will come. There will be plenty of glitter.)

Imagine the home team is the good guys: organizations working to improve the lives of LGBTIQ people around the world, organizations like the International Gay and Lesbian Human Rights Commission (IGLHRC)... *go team!* The opposing team is the bad guys: organizations fighting against equality at an international level, organizations like the Alliance Defending Freedom (ADF)—*boo!*

The home team has a few plays used to try and score equality. One is called the "Day of Silence," promoting awareness of the effects of bullying on LGBT people by asking students to take a vow of silence in support of schools addressing the problem of anti-LGBT behavior. The organization responsible for the "Day of Silence" works hard to stop bullying.

The ADF has its playbook, too though, and hosts a "Day of Truth." This day was created in response to a high school student's suspension for wearing a T-shirt reading *Be Ashamed—Homosexuality is Shameful*. The ADF works hard to promote the opportunity to wear that shirt.

There are also defensive plays: IGLHRC works to disassemble systemic inequalities and promote economic, social, and cultural rights, such as working against the use of government facilities to host conversion therapy seminars in South Korea.

And ADF is pushing back, entrenching discrimination by carving out exemptions from nondiscrimination laws, as it did when advising supporters of Russian antigay legislation.

These organizations seem like opposite forces, so much so that one ADF brief submitted during an Italian lawsuit on marriage equality calls out these converse perspectives for LGBT civil rights: "While this Court has suggested that an emerging consensus exists toward legal recognition of same-sex relationships, reality suggests that an equally strong countertrend toward recognizing marriage as exclusively between one man and one woman exists."[1]

What if the growth of this countermovement is tied to LGBT progress?

One leader of a UK-based international LGBT organization says, "If you look at the history of the advancement of LGBT rights in the UK, every advance is accompanied by a backlash."[2]

---

[1] Third Party Intervention by Alliance Defending Freedom in *Orlandi and Others v. Italy*, Application No. 26431/12 before the Second Section of the European Court of Human Rights. http://adfinternational.org/2014/02/14/orlandi-and-others-v-italy/

[2] Alistair Stewart, officer at the Kaleidoscope Trust. Quoted by Saner, Emine. "Gay rights around the world: the best and worst countries for equality." *The Guardian*, 30 July 2013.

If history has taught us anything, it's that the drum beats slowly for civil rights.

Imagine standing at the precipice of everything that has happened for LGBT rights—good and bad. What should you think about the progress of the LGBT movement?

If you look down, you see gay characters on TV shows (on prime time)! Your newsfeed is filled with hopeful stories as celebrities and companies support equal rights and pay and employment. You see the US Supreme Court's ruling on marriage equality on June 26, 2015.

If you look up, though—beyond your own newsfeed, optimized to show news you agree with—you might see that on June 27, 2015, US states began creative disobedience. You might see seventy-nine countries, with a combined population of over three billion, still criminalizing homosexuality. You might see the closet still crowded with people who have their backs to the exit, or notice the corner of that closet where bodies stack up in silence.

Change has not come fast. It's a long road to equality. So, with all that progress and anti-progress, the question is simple: are you content with the pace of change?

If you are satisfied, it must only be after understanding its cost: the pain caused by laws, and fists, and words on real people who don't get the respite of change in their lifetime. Because change is slow. Entire lives will come and go before Perfect Equality is realized.

---

http://www.theguardian.com/world/2013/jul/30/gay-rights-world-best-worst-countries

If you are *not* satisfied, if you are *not* willing to accept inequality's accumulating harm… how far would you go to reach equality faster?

The Scales of Justice

Chapter 14

Love Crimes

There wasn't even a breath between the thug rolling up his sleeve to reveal a Mission Morality tattoo and the erection sprouting up beneath him. The force of the concrete cock created a horrible crack when it bulged beneath the man's ribcage, but it was the wet splat of his head on the pavement that made me vomit.

"There, there. Not on the equipment, please." The queen's clip-on nails tapped my back, but her eyes stayed glued to the monitor.

She cheered as Dildee, the man conjuring concrete penises, stepped around a corner to greet the cowering boy he'd saved.

"It's okay." A jewelry store's hacked security camera let us see and hear Dildee from our control room. "You're safe now."

Wiping his nose with the cuff of his hoodie, the boy smeared blood across his cheek.

"What the fuck?" A second Mission Morality thug examined

his friend's unmoving body sprawled next to an erect statue in the middle of the street. "What did you do?! You fucking killed him!"

He fired a few shots into the air and pointed his gun at Dildee's back. The boy dropped back into the fetal position while our operative positioned himself between them.

"Uh oh." The queen giggled, twisting a knob that zoomed into the unsuspecting thug. "What con-*cock*-shun's up next?!"

"God. Can you at least fake it?" Adele barked.

The scene played out on the control room monitor while Adele handed me a towel. Dildee tapped his cane on the ground, and equality inched forward as two concrete statues crushed harm like a pimple.

The queen cheered. "We need some popcorn for this shit! Can we get that on replay?"

"Christ, you're heartless." Adele sounded disgusted, a different kind of sick than what I'd left on the control room floor.

"Can't hold this back." The queen started reading from a separate screen. "Ronald Rodgers, Mission Morality member: two counts verbal assault; active involvement in planning the Tribeca Raid; murdered a transgender woman last week; and would have got another were it not for Dildee's *stiff* resistance."

Adele waved her off and helped me outside as I tried to keep what I hadn't already spewed in until the door shut behind us. Outside the control room, we melted against the wall.

"This is crazy, right?" I asked. "I mean, what we saw. That's crazy."

"Crazy's just come to the surface," Adele said.

"You sound like her. I knew this was a bad idea."

"They started it." Adele said, convincing herself or believing it outright. "Watching makes it real. It's easy to forget what happens after we meet."

"Yeah." I laughed. "Concrete cocks killing homophobes. That shit's real as fuck."

We entered the glass elevator, and my stomach jumped for my throat as we descended through clouds, down hundreds of floors, to the city below.

"What are we doing?" I asked.

"Stopped pretending it's okay. That's all."

"We promised to be honest. No debate, and Jesus, no morality equations. Just tell me… does it *feel* like we're doing good?"

Adele took a minute to think. "It's hard to remember how we got here, but I can. Mission Morality is killing us. This is the only reasonable response."

"Utility Positive," I verbalized the verdict of the Scales of Justice—our first decision that had not been unanimous.

"Right."

If wished I could choose Adele's perspective. To think we *had* made the right decision. To think that if the whole world came to the conclusion that everything was fucked up, that it would finally be an adequate response to the way things had always been. But, perspective exists from fixed points.

The red sun set out of view behind us, casting the Ivory Tower's endless shadow straight down Main Street. As we approached the ground floor the sounds of the party, which accompanied every Renegayd mission, seeped through the elevator doors. My excuses began as the elevator slowed.

"Not in the mood tonight. Think I'm gonna get some sleep."

Adele squinted. "You're still looking for him, aren't you?"

"I—" There was no point in lying. "I want to make sure he's okay."

"Transplant, Blank Canvas, member of the Scales of Justice... you could have anyone you want, Sam. What's with this guy?"

"He'd say those are my top offenses."

Adele sighed. "Make sure you get some sleep. By tomorrow morning we'll have killed thousands of people."

With a shrug of exhaustion, she headed toward the party's temporary numbness, leaving me to search for Brun-Brun. Finding him had become more hopeless after months of futile searching, but doing so let me feel the fullness of what I'd gotten myself into: *war*—one that would bring LGBT liberation or destroy everything in trying.

Chapter 1

Spin Spin Spin

My neighbor Walter wasn't allowed to eat sugary cereals. Childhood karma would destine him to grow up, grow out, and get diabetes... but actually, he's a lawyer. He goes to the gym every morning and married his high school sweetheart.

Childhood karma is remarkably unfulfilling. More often than not, bullies don't end up in prison, quarterbacks don't peak, and bookish shy kids become socially awkward adults. It never plays out like you hope, fortunate considering the dumb reasons I'd wished horrible lives on people. Refusing to share a fruit roll-up shouldn't warrant a life of misery.

That's not to say Walter didn't rebel. The moment his mom told him he was forbidden to eat cookies for breakfast, a part of him could think of nothing else. Every time Walter came over, he'd start and end his visit with a heaping bowl of Cookie Crisp.

Sugary cereal is cute. Sexual promiscuity—apparently—is not.

"Go to club, leave with stranger" doesn't conjure the same warm tingle as stories of Walter's hand in the Count Chocula box. How different are they, though? A shot of insulin or a shot of penicillin.

The world was my grocery store aisle. Look, but don't touch, don't think, don't wonder, don't fantasize... come to think of it, better not look.

So, while everyone was helping themselves—a taste in elementary, a first real serving in middle school, and a splurge in high school—I was fasting. Hopelessly splurgeless, my neighbor's pantry became the World Wide Web. Walter got the better deal. He enjoyed his forbidden fruit in the comforts of my pantry. I looked at pictures of Froot Loops until I Honey Nut.

Despite my Internet history, it took years for me to accept I was gay. When I did, I felt downright pathetic. I'd never had a real sexual experience. Sure, I'd felt my friend's boob. Once! But that was clinical at best. Like feeling an avocado to test if it's ready for guacamole. (It would never be.)

But college.... college would be my liberation. College meant gays lining the quad, tanning their muscular bodies after a hard workout.

I had seen so much porn. How could this not work?

What they don't tell you about Notre Dame is that the gays aren't exactly lining the quad. How could I have known? I mean, the brochures circumvented details on gay student life, but I hadn't expected ND admissions to advertise like a gay cruise line. Gays were a given. This was college!

Turns out, omission was the gentle reflection of the school's refusal to recognize gays in any way. Not Our Lady of the Lake!

Our Lady swims in a one-piece and waits until marriage... nay, she doesn't even do that. She doesn't have sex with anyone but God, and even then it's immaculate.

Needless to say, my cereal bowl remained empty.

What would have happened to Walter if he didn't sneak Fruity Pebbles from my pantry? What if instead, every time Walter thought about sugary cereal he found the door locked and the aisle empty, God and his mother ringing in his head?

It's not that big a deal—cereal—but when you want it, and you know other people are having it, and its photograph is used to sell everything from underwear to cell phones, what do you think that does to a person?

Boxes of cereal prancing around the quad. Look at me! Look at me! Sugar Smacks caught a Frisbee! Apple Jacks does musical theater! Let's get drunk with Golden Grahams! Too much wanting makes Walter a little hornball. He's gonna have that cereal, and he might just overindulge. He don't care. Walter's a loose, cereal cannon. You don't know. You don't know!

But sugary cereal is *cute*. Reaching college without kissing someone you're attracted to is sad. Worse. *Dirty, dangerous, gross, forbidden...* those are the descriptors gays are raised to associate with sex.

Spoiler: I eventually had sex. Thanks to a lack of childhood karma, my romp through the world of gay sex did not doom me forever. Instead it brought me to San Francisco as a well-adjusted, gainfully employed, recently single, out gay man.

But who am I kidding? Those years of fasting affect everything.

For one, being recently single meant my best friend Jacob

(the new Walter) was dead set on helping me rebound.

"Come on!" he urged.

Jacob pulled me down Seventeenth Street's steep grade as if I might escape, were he not my anchor.

"I don't know. I've got work tomorrow. I'm already going to have a hangover," I said.

"Exactly! Too late to turn back. Musical Mondays can't be less intimidating: nothing but drinks and musical belting. *And no-body in allll of Oz.*" We both knew when I left my apartment I'd lost the right to turn back. "*No wizard that there is or was. Is....*"

His smile grew goofier in the pause, before I joined in.

"*Everrr gonna bring meeeee dowww-nnn!!*"

We sprinted the rest of the way down Seventeenth, turned right on Castro, and were at The Edge in less than five minutes. This was my San Francisco. A smorgasbord of gay living the BK life, having it our way. From gym to zoo, we were all accounted for: bears, otters, cubs, twinks, jocks, the recently single, and instigating friends.

"All That Jazz" and "Don't Cry For Me, Argentina" unite the masses.

Jacob focused on my rebound. A few years ago this would have been up my alley, but a serious relationship dulled once-valuable skills like pounding shots and cruising bars.

"Come *on!*" Jacob pulled me in the door. "What do you want? First one's on me."

"Anchor Steam." I shouted, above "Chim Chim Cher-ee."

Jacob slipped his way to the front of the line with a combination of muscle and flirting, while I found us a spot in view of the screens playing clips for each song.

Monday nights belonged to The Edge. The place was packed, and yet the inebriated crowd still managed every chorus in more harmony than if the Marina was hosting. Everyone was entranced by their own passionate performance.

The corner table held a strange juxtaposition with the atmosphere: light-skin, dark-hair, lips pursed—brooding—a handsome twentysomething disengaged from the warbling around him. He was hot, and he was staring at me. Nerves greased my rusted gears to kick off the night with bumbling game. Instead of responding with a cheesy grin, or a wave, I just stared back.

"Hey!" Jacob bumped into me as if spit back out from the bar. "*Heeyyy*. 'Not ready for this' my ass. Got you a long island. Seems like you're back in the saddle fine without it. Go talk to him!"

"Come on! Not my type."

"So?" he said. "Go on!"

Jacob shoved me forward, but before I could consider making a move, a wall of ripped deltoids and the back of a blond crew cut intercepted my target.

I turned around. "If that's his type, it wasn't going to work anyway."

"Hold up. Look!"

Jacob spun me back around as the huge, blond man shoved the brooding boy. They exchanged shouts, squaring off for a minute, before the boy deflated, ceding his table to the asshole meathead.

"That guy should be kicked out of here!" I said.

I watched the exit for another glimpse of the hottie, who

looked at the ground as he left. The buff blond had taken up the corner and was already chatting up someone new.

"You want to console him... in your mouth?" Jacob teased. "Plenty other fish in the sea."

One long island was all it took for my mood and inhibitions to lift, but I pushed straight past calm, cool, and collected.

"Nan sin-quein yah! Sebedi sebeda!"

My feet gained weight, and my body slowed as Mufasa's chanting ran into *Newsies* and *Spring Awakening*. The singing borrowed momentum from the drinking. I was feeling good. It had been a long time since I'd gone this big.

"You know what time it is?" I shouted. "Time for Badlands!"

Jacob squealed in delight. "Sam! Couple drinks and you go from enabled to enabler. Love it!" We headed next door to get in the short line. "You're lucky I don't have a job, or you wouldn't have any company for your weekday romp through the 'Stro!"

"Don't remind me. The last thing I want to think about is the hungover workday waiting for me."

"Deal," said Jacob. "You don't remind me I'm unemployed, and I won't remind you you're squandering all your opportunities."

We showed our IDs to the bouncer and entered the bar that acted like a hallway to the main stage. The rainbow pop nightclub smelled like sweaty Monday night partiers.

"I've got this one!"

I headed for the bar. We were already waking up with a headache. No point in stopping now. Badlands was less crowded than The Edge; those who weren't rebounding had gone home for the night.

"Two long islands!"

I bopped to the consistent beat.

"Twenty bucks."

A hand on my shoulder stopped me reaching for my wallet.

"I've got it."

My heart leaped. He was back! The dark-haired boy from The Edge nodded at the bartender, who nodded back, then went to someone else's order. That, *I'm familiar enough with the bartender to get a drink with a nod*, was one more reason he wasn't my type.

Worry not: logic was easily cast aside by hormones and alcohol.

"Oh! Hey. You!" It had been a while since I'd picked someone up. "I'm Sam."

His sulky smirk stretched thin, and I realized the pickup had already happened. He got me a drink, and I accepted. That's enough for a Monday night.

"Jacques."

He gave me a hug, his cologne—probably French—sweet and masculine. During the quick embrace our bodies ignited. His hand swept up my back until his fingertips curled in my hair. Heat stirred between us, and when we separated his hand brushed my crotch.

The casual brush: not something most straights are familiar with, because the idea of a man going up to a woman for a fistful of boob was unimaginable. Still, in Badlands on a Monday night, the feeling of his hand brushing my jeans got a smile.

He said something too drenched in accent and bass for me to understand.

"What?" I shouted.

"Want to get out of here?"

Before responding, I looked for Jacob. He was on the dance floor, watching. Our eyes met, and his enthusiastic mouthing told me what to do, *GO! GO!* Acquaintances go to bars with you; good friends never leave you behind; and best friends encourage you to leave them.

"Sure," I said, but his casual brush had already told him everything he needed to know.

He smirked... again. The effect hadn't worn off, and we left. Outside, the San Francisco air reduced my drunkenness, the cool fog casting its night prolonging spell.

"Try to follow me." Jacques said, complete with rolled "r" and shortened vowels.

"Shouldn't be too hard."

My own giddiness embarrassed me. Hand in hand we ran down Eighteenth Street toward Castro. He grabbed the pole mounting the stoplight above the gayest corner in the world and spun around.

"Come. Ow about you try. Spin wiz me."

Caught up in the mystery and silliness of the night, I grabbed the pole below his hand and watched him across from me. He surprised me, and I liked that. It helped defend against the feeling that this was a horrible decision. Together, we spun around the pole, faster and faster. I laughed, and he said something strange.

"Spin spin spin. To the world within."

When he said "Within," Castro Street folded over on itself. Like a pop-up book, Nineteenth Street uprooted, pointing Castro up to the sky before the block up-corner replanted itself on top of Eighteenth Street. The rainbow crosswalk folded beneath the new site, which existed beneath Castro, revealed by the page turn.

"Wha—?" I stopped spinning, holding my head. "Think maybe I drank too much. Did you?"

Jacques didn't react. *How much did I drink?*

"Come on. I've got Advil."

He seemed cool, so I nodded. For some reason, I just nodded. The street was crowded, more alive than I imagined a Monday night should be, but I hadn't been out like this in a long time. Everything felt different.

My eyes stayed glued to Jacques's. Face-to-face, my mind processed what a strange hookup this was while my feet trudged after the bait. There was doubt. Couldn't I still stop? But Jacques was hot as hell, more beautiful in moonlight than Badlands strobe.

"I don't recognize this," I managed, referencing every building in my peripheral vision.

Jacques's voice called my attention back. "It's right here."

We were at his front door.

"Wow," I said. "Central."

He leaned in, reigniting the fire between us, and kissed me. His lips were cold, the opposite of what I imagined, making me hotter. I reached under his shirt, feeling his stomach, reaching lower.

"Wait," he said, separating us.

He was different. Pupils glowing, stranded in a sea-green ocean. Skin lighter, thin blue veins running across his cheeks and temple.

"Are you—?"

"Kiss me," he instructed.

My body was happy to obey, but my mind raced to dissect the sudden change of his voice. How many voices did he have?

He pushed the door open.

"Follow me."

Up the stairs it was difficult to keep from jumping him as he fiddled with his door lock. But it didn't feel like self-control that kept me from acting. Standing at the threshold, feeling nothing but lust and fear, I stared motionless at my rebound. He took his time hanging his keys on a peg, looking up to gift a smile that raised my attention. He was at ease, and I wrestled the carnal signals in his doorway.

Fight, flight, or sex. No wonder people think gays are evolutionary appendages.

Jacques removed his coat. His loose T-shirt was tucked into the front of his jeans, and my imagination toyed with what lay beneath his demon-face belt buckle. I needed to ravage him, or at least to explore that beautiful body.

"Go to the bed," he ordered.

Finally! I crossed the living area to the foot of his bed and turned around to wait.

He thanked me by grabbing the bottom of his shirt to peel it off. Jacques transformed with every inch revealed. His skin turned pale—inhuman—but his shape was perfect. A fit and toned V tugged my gaze down, and his shirt continued lifting, up and over his head. Had his hair always been silver?

I still recognized the boy who'd caught my gaze, but he was also something else. It didn't matter; both were gorgeous. At the foot of his bed I longed to see more, throbbed for his touch. I wanted to run to him, press our bodies back together, taste his skin, slip beneath that belt buckle. But I waited, soaking up his beauty.

Lust overpowered fear.

"Your shirt," he said.

His lips curled while my hands fumbled, and by the time I'd ripped it off he was next to me. Even without touching I felt his chill. His body was foreign, threatening, perfect.

A whisper of frigid air caressed my cheek. His tongue an ice cube, dripping down my neck to my chest. I shivered when he kissed my nipple. I couldn't move, not until he told me. He was doing the work anyway, unzipping my fly.

In one quick motion he hooked my cock out with an ice-cold finger and pressed his body against mine. I let out a little moan, unable to contain the pleasure I felt when the tip of me stood over his waistline and pressed against our stomachs. He unbuttoned my jeans and pushed them to my ankles.

"The bed," he said with a thousand voices.

I fell backward. Jacques pressed his bulge against me, and I managed to get his jeans over his ass so that we touched. The sensation of fire and ice fueled my desire. He was magnificent. I dug my fingers into his back and kissed his neck.

I wanted him more than anyone I'd ever been with, the strangeness not escaping me, but trampled by more insistent needs.

"Look up," he said, and my gaze slid from his inhuman features to the ceiling of his apartment. My body concentrated on other senses, soaking up the chill of his breath as he moved past my belly button.

Even his smell was different. Like burnt pine, sexy in pure uniqueness.

There was a crashing sound inside the apartment, but Jacques wrapped his lips around me and dragged his hand after as he descended. I was not going to stop this to mention the noise. Obedient, I stared upward as his chill engulfed me.

A brilliant white light cast new shadows on the ceiling, warmth rushing over me except for what he sheltered. My gaze broke from the ceiling, and I looked down at Jacques. Someone stood behind him, inside the light.

"STOP THIS!" a deep voice boomed.

Jacques screeched, more like a rat than a human, and scurried to the corner of the room. I blinked, struggling to see through the radiance until it dimmed. As it did, I realized my body wasn't warm at all. I was shivering, inside and out.

Jacques cowered in the corner, covering his face with both arms, hands wrapped around the back of his neck. Then he darted across the room and grabbed a piece of paper from his dresser.

"Permit!" Jacques shrieked. "Permitted feeding!"

The fluorescence dissipated, its source revealed as bulging deltoids and a blond crew cut.

"You dumbass," he said. "Persistent aren't you? I broke this sucker once, and you had to find him again."

"What?" My erect cock bobbed as I sat up.

"Let's get out of here." He continued, turning to the shivering body in the corner. "You stay there, 'k?"

"My head," I said. "What happened?"

"Alcohol," he said. "That's on you. Let's get out of here. From the looks of it, you have no problem following instructions."

I hated the way he looked at me. I didn't strip down for him. It was violating. I pulled my pants back up, certain that whatever had been interrupted was worse than this alternative. The attraction between Jacques and I was gone; something broke between us.

Waiting outside the apartment I heard the meathead tell Jacques, "Not this one. K?" Then he followed me out. "Go on downstairs. Unless you want me to leave you two alone again? Geez, you look terrible."

"What the hell is going on? I'm not going anywhere. What is this place? What happened in there? Who are you?"

My blond savior was not impressed. "*Now* you wanna fight. A second ago you were spread-eagle, game for anything. Sometimes I think the suckers would make the best Sentries. Get people to waltz wherever they want, if they weren't so horned up all the time."

"Please!"

He laughed again as we stepped into the street, and I hated him even more for that reaction to my despair.

The Castro was gone. Something *had* happened back at the pole at Eighteenth and Castro. The city had transformed, replaced by something different.

"What?" I examined the new pointy roofs across from me. "What the hell happened to the city?"

"First, things first. I'm Brun-Brun—Sentry Brun-Brun—and you're welcome for saving you." He waited for my thanks, which I was happy to withhold. "Alrighty... well you're clearly not in Kansas anymore. You put that much together?"

"Then where am I?"

"Pole doesn't spin for anyone, Sam. In portmanteau, we call it Gantasy, Garadise, or my favorite, Gatlantis."

"Can you please answer my question?"

"Not a word masher... Gay Fantasy? Gay Paradise? Gay Atlantis?" Brun-Brun waited for me to respond. "Nothing? Geez. Gist is, you're home."

Chapter 15

Making Lemonade

Love Crimes was a success. Even refusing to support it, I'd known the equation would turn out Utility Positive. They always did. Debate of that fact was reserved to our meeting room high in the Ivory Tower. The Scales of Justice existed to spread confidence; that way, the lack of it was confined to the six members.

Laughter seeped into the hall when I entered the Scales of Justice room, betraying the somber expressions painted on my fellow members. Jacob was sharing news about his first foursome, and Benj had to cut off his howl when he saw me at the entrance.

"It was my first!" Jacob laughed, resolved to finish his story. "Thought it was worth sharing."

"Everyone okay?" I said.

Adele gave me a sad smile. "We're okay."

"I'm great! Love Crimes was a total success. Utility Positive!" Jacob pointed at the chalkboard with the equation that proved it. The one I'd refused to support. "We're all doing great."

"Then why isn't anyone looking me in the eye?"

Jacob met my challenge with anger. "We don't have to apologize for seeing good. We *saved* lives! You can wallow in being the one who refused Love Crimes, but don't you dare say 'I told you so.' If you'd had your way, it would be lives on our side—more of them. And that would be on your hands."

When he finished, I asked my real question. "How bad was it? How many?"

Jacob sat back down. He must have thought I'd already known.

Shǎng answered. "More than ten thousand. Most of them Mission Morality and sympathizers."

"Wow." I braced myself against the back of a chair. "Ten thousand."

"More saved," Jacob said. "Why not ask, How *good* was it? How many hate crimes did we stop? How many people did we bring back to the Ivory Tower to arm with Spectrum abilities? How many future lives were improved by hastening our path to Perfect Equality?"

"I get it, Jacob," I said. "I heard the debate."

A glitter-apparition shimmered between us, and I saw the group through a kaleidoscope before it solidified into the queen, a puddle of glitter beneath her feet. Her azure dress accentuated her black skin.

"I hope spirits are *high*!" she sang. "We did it."

"I don't want credit for this," I said.

"Oh hush, Broccolini." She gave her wand a curious jiggle and a newspaper slipped out. "Total Victory." She jiggled again, and another fell out of her wand. "Gays Fight Back." A third slipped out, which she grabbed to read more than the headline. "Mission Morality heightens attacks. Renegayd responds. Renegayd members intervened in tens of thousands of hate crimes around the world. While deaths were reported on both sides, Mission Morality incurred the overwhelming majority." She looked up. "Inaction would certainly have resulted in thousands of LGBT deaths."

"Gay liberation day," Jacob said. "That's how this will be remembered. In memory of the Renegayd members who lost their lives fighting for equality. We promised to make a difference, and yesterday's the most tangible example yet."

"We orchestrated the whole thing!" I couldn't help myself. "If we hadn't told the world we were going to be patrolling for hate crimes, there wouldn't have been so many to stop. And you said 'yet!' What's next? This escalation's a race to the bottom."

"It was Utility Positive." Jacob looked to the others for support. "He doesn't have to see it."

"You don't want to discuss it?" I said. "We killed thousands of people, and you're over it?"

"We signed off on Love Crimes," Jacob continued. "You may not feel the good, but the people we saved do. Not to mention the message we sent the next asshole thinking about ganging up on some poor soul. We helped that kid avoid a beating, and that's enough for me. Can we please move on?"

Jacob looked at the queen, but she was staring at me.

"If he's got something to say," she ceded, "he should say it."

"How many families did we shatter? Husbands, wives, parents, children killed by Renegayd because they were too fucking stupid to understand that equality's got nothing to do with them."

"We're doing right," Jacob said. "It's complicated, but it's right."

Working with the Scales was difficult. Sleepless nights were hard, but they didn't compare to the mind fuck rewiring that let me see utility in wagering a friendship. Fighting with Jacob—even if it cost me my best friend—was worth it. So, I tried re-explaining what I'd failed to before the group had otherwise unanimously supported the queen's plan, starting with the equation Jacob used as some ironclad crutch.

"If there's no limit to what Mission Morality will do, then our equation is too flexible."

"We agreed not to rehash things we've already decided," Jacob tried. "It's messy, but we need to make progress."

"This is our chance to be the voice of reason. We have the world's sympathy."

"*Had*," the queen said, proud of herself. "You been so absorbed in all this that you missed the real news. The third way. A group called the Global Rights Organization. They're all over the news denouncing Love Crimes. Calling for a peaceful resolution between Renegayd and Mission Morality."

"Yer kiddin'," Benj said.

The queen flopped her wand around, materializing a luminescent window, which somehow showed live news from back home. The ticker running across the bottom read, *Rift in LGBT Support. Global Rights Organization Comes Out against*

Renegayd. Above it, a man stood at a podium, the label beneath reading, *Apollo Vazquez.*

"Mr. Vazquez," a reporter questioned from off screen, "don't you worry this will slow things down? By your own words, you agree with Renegayd's goal. Aren't you worried the Global Rights Organization will fracture that cause?"

Apollo Vazquez spoke softly. "Thank you for the question. Let me be clear. We aren't fracturing the goal of equality, because at the center of that goal is human dignity and love. Renegayd stands for neither. They've shown their center contains the same hatred as Mission Morality. This new Global Rights Organization—an organization of our own world—offers the real solution, a nonviolent solution. Hatred does not cease by hatred, but by love; this is the eternal rule."

The queen popped the window back out of existence.

"And more like that," she said. "Feel better, Sugar Cupcake? Got your voice of reason."

"We did that," Jacob said.

Benj was beaming. Why were we celebrating a rational organization bashing us?

"We have to meet with them," I said.

The queen popped her hand on her hip and recoiled. "We just declared war on Mission Morality. We killed thousands of people! We're the megaphone."

"This is our chance! We can lead the movement for equality!" I said.

Impassioned, the queen responded more to the room than to me. "We stay true to what we created: a fight for equality. For radical love. This is not about Us-versus-Them opinion polls.

Renegayd set out to transform the world. The Global Rights Organization will play it slow, and while they do, Mission Morality will murder us. For gay rights, it's violence that takes courage. The rest will follow suit." Her tone lightened. "Y'all do what you want with the plans I bring you. I'll honor your conclusion. Who am I to question the great Scales of Justice?" Jazz hands. "But you do not make the plans for Renegayd."

The Global Rights Organization confirmed a feeling I'd felt growing for months, that we were as much of the problem as Mission Morality. Our violence might have created the Global Rights Organization, but now that it existed, Renegayd was no longer the path to equality.

"We need to meet with the Global Rights Organization," I said.

"We don't make the plans," Benj restated. "She brings 'em. We debate 'em."

I walked to the chalkboard, picked up a piece of chalk, and drew an "A" next to the equation deeming Love Crimes to be Utility Positive.

"Ahh yes. A new variable. That will fix everything!" Jacob scoffed.

"This 'A' represents the alternative. That's what the Global Rights Organization represents, an alternative path to Perfect Equality, one that isn't eye for an eye. Support the Global Rights Organization, and we can reach equality through peace."

"Why are you not understanding our role?" Jacob said, looking at the queen as she watched our debate. "We do not make the plans."

"Fine. You don't want to meet with the Global Rights

Organization? Try rationalizing Love Crimes again." I circled the equation, including my big 'A.' "How much good does this alternative represent?"

Nobody said anything.

"What are you sayin'?" Benj finally asked.

"I get it," Adele said. "I don't have a clue what that variable represents... what the Global Rights Organization represents. So, how can we take action? We agreed the right action is the one that causes the most good—more than other possibilities. The Global Rights Organization is a very real possibility, and we can't say how it affects our equation until we check."

I looked straight at the queen, realizing that if treason was a thing here, I was dangerously close. "*This* blocks almost every plan you could come up with. So long as there's a real alternative, the utility of our actions can be questioned."

"Love Crimes was hard," Adele said. "But it was good because it avoided more harm than it caused. It sped our path to equality. I know we did the right thing, but had the Global Rights Organization existed then—when we were debating it—I don't know if I could have supported it."

Our equations were all contrived, valuable only as a thought experiment to focus our conversations. We swapped things around, threw astronomical values into each variable, and tested the outcomes. They were never perfect, but the grey areas didn't bother me. It was the lack of them that did. Mission Morality's actions made things so black and white that every equation easily swung in our favor.

Benj thought out loud. "Couldn't we have thrown that 'A' on the board even before the Global Rights Organization? I mean, there's plenty of things we could've done other than Love Crimes, but it was the plan in front of us."

"There's countless deviations from any one plan too," said Shǎng. "Like, bombing an innocent city is bad, but drawing a big middle finger on the bomb that hits the city is slightly, *slightly* worse."

"This is different," I said. "The Global Rights Organization is a significant alternative. A new element to the equation, not a different shade of something else."

The queen stood in front of the floor-to-ceiling window, looking at the cloud-city beneath. Somewhere farther down was the actual city. She didn't seem pleased, but we paused for her reaction out of instinct.

"Ready for distribution?" she asked.

"Wait." The queen was full of surprises. "You'll meet with them?"

"Meeting with the Global Rights Organization will prove how slow their path to equality truly is. Then you can pump that into your equations. I won't allow Renegayd to make the same mistake other groups have made. Every minute we're not fighting to reduce inequality's harm we become accessories to it. If one meeting gets this out of your system, I want to do it fast."

That wasn't the whole reason. She knew that if *I* thought the Global Rights Organization was an opportunity, others would too. For once, her need for popularity worked for us. I scribbled the new equation on a piece of paper and looked desperately at the rest of the group. The queen was taking our advice for the first time. It was now or never, before she changed her mind.

"Fuck. Fine," Jacob said.

The queen transformed my scrawl into calligraphy, adding the glossy finish she gave all our decisions. Then, with her wand against the glass window, she brought the elaborate flier to its back end.

"Queen of Witches got one chat in me. Then we're back to it. K?"

She touched the flier to her wand. It was sucked up and spit back out on the opposite side of the glass. In transport, it multiplied into thousands of identical messages fluttering toward the city like carrier pigeons at the end of a long journey, gliding down to spread news of Renegayd's next step.

Dionysia, the Queen of Witches, evaporated, a twinkling puddle the only proof she'd been with us at all. I released a breath I hadn't realized I'd been holding.

"Wow," Adele said.

"Stupid." Jacob stormed out.

Our decision fell through the clouds, raining confidence on the city below. Renegayd would meet a third party who sought equality through nonviolence, and for the first time in a long time, I was proud to be on the Scales of Justice.

Chapter 2

The Queen of Witches

Brun-Brun looked at a clock wrapped in a pink feather boa on one of the buildings, and his steps quickened.

"Mind if we pick up the pace? She hates when we're late."

"Happy to… if you'll tell me where we're going. Who are you even talking about?" Brun-Brun clearly didn't want to hurt me. Whatever creature we left behind might have killed me, were it not for him.

"The Queen of Witches," he said.

"Queen… of Witches?"

"She picked the name. Dionysia, if you want to be informal."

We were walking down what had been Castro Street before the transformation. Without Jacques's trance, I saw the city's full metamorphosis—awake to the dreamland I'd entered by spinning around the pole at Eighteenth and Castro.

Harvey's, the Sausage Factory, Cliff's, everything had been

replaced with... other things. Strange things. A bright orange market where Q-Bar used to be; the embossed, emerald name above its door read, *Whatever*.

Whatever Whatever sold was popular. A line stretched three doors down, and examining the people made me see the Castro's transformation as amplification. The first four people in line each had a different colored handkerchief in their back pockets. I counted four miniature Chihuahuas: one attached to a black purse held by a sailor boy wearing aviators; another held by a woman in camo; and the last two on diamond leashes in the right and left hands of a purple-haired, shirtless stud. That was not the first time I'd seen any of it, just all of it together.

"It's not far." Brun-Brun pointed ahead, and my jaw dropped.

Market and Castro had been replaced by a colossal tower. Its white facade stretched endlessly up to the unperceivable top floor, creating a near blinding reflection as I craned backwards to take it all in. A solid-white wall surrounded the tower with one visible entry point, an open gate. Running along the wall, a garden of flowering bushes was trimmed into suggestive shapes. Two rose bushes were trained from their bases to bow away from each other before rejoining at the top, creating a beautiful, undisguised vagina that climbed a quarter of the way up the wall.

"What is that?"

"Just noticing?" he said. "That's the Ivory Tower. Most of it's empty, but she likes the spectacle."

"*That* is empty?"

"Not entirely. The queen lives there. Others come and go, but it's so big."

"Wow." I laughed. "It's... a lot."

"You'll see." Brun-Brun put his arm around me and squeezed.

We walked beneath the iron gateway and beyond the white wall, making me wonder if the transformation had affected more than the Castro. Two women opened the tower door as we approached.

"Hey, Brun-Brun. What you got there?" one of them squawked.

"Fresh blood!" he said, and then turned to me, looking panicked. "I'm kidding! We work together. Geez. Don't worry."

"Glad you find this hilarious," I said.

"You'll get used to it," he said. "All the Transplants do."

"I'm going to get tired of asking this... but what do you mean?"

He smacked my back. "You weren't born here! So, you're a Transplant."

"You were?" It didn't seem possible. This was the other side of the Castro.

"Yup. For me, the shock was how things are on your side. Least we've got a good surprise for you."

The tower's ivory doors led to an entryway that compressed all the exterior gaudiness into one outrageous room. The first thing visible inside the tower—of course—was a rainbow. Its full arch stretched across the room ending at large, ornate doors on each side, rather than pots of gold. Above the left door, a neon yellow sign read, *The Spectrum*. The right bore gemstone calligraphy on the door itself: *Queen of Witches*.

A waterfall cascaded from above the rainbow, straight through its midpoint into a pool feeding a river, which divided the room in half. The thunder that should have emanated from the indoor falls was a soft whir. The mist, which refracted the full rainbow, should have made the room feel wet, but it felt crisp. A bridge crossed the river at its mouth, and the whole flamboyant thing appeared to be constructed around the rainbow centerpiece.

We took the right path through the rainbow mist towards the bejeweled, *Queen of Witches* door. Brun-Brun took post at its side.

"That's the one you want," he said.

"You're not coming?"

"I see her plenty. She likes to talk to the Transplants alone. I'll be right here."

Disappointed and suddenly frightened, I examined the door. "Where's the handle?"

Brun-Brun wasn't fazed. "Let it know what you want," he said.

A lifetime spent marinating in this world clearly dulled his senses to these eccentricities.

"What does that mean?" I asked.

"Exactly what it sounds."

"Fine." I squared up to the doorway. "I want to see the queen."

I looked at Brun-Brun, who stood silently, and then back at the door. I half expected a door handle to appear out of nowhere.

"It's not working," I said, and Brun-Brun nodded. So, I shouted, "I WANT TO SEE THE QUEEN OF WITCHES."

"No you don't." The high-pitched voice came from the door, but there was no discernable change in its appearance.

"EXCUSE ME?" I said.

"You heard me... we heard you. So stop shouting," the door said back. "You don't want to see the queen."

"Yeah!" a different, higher-pitched voice screeched. "You're just saying it."

"Um. No, I really do want to see her." I was blushing.

"He's a liar!"

"LIAR!"

"Pants on fire!"

A chorus of shrill voices berated me, accompanied—I suddenly realized—by tiny flickers in the gemstones.

"Where are you?" I asked.

"We're right here, you faker," said one.

I looked at the door, something was definitely strange about it, but I didn't see anyone talking.

"CLOSER!" one screeched.

I leaned closer, and the movement became more prominent. It wasn't the gemstones, but something inside them.

"Take a picture!"

"It'll last longer!"

Inside each stone was a tiny creature, each the color of its gem, with large, bald heads, wide eyes, and thin arms pounding on their inner walls as they jabbered.

"Amazing," I said, half to myself and half to Brun-Brun. "They're little aliens."

"Ehehehe." "Heheha!" "Heheh!"

"We're fairies!"

"Like you!"

Of course they were fairies. What else would be at the end of a rainbow inside this place?

"Doors don't open without you opening them." They were less helpful than Brun-Brun.

"I can't open it without a handle." I wasn't sure whether to argue with one of them or the whole group.

"If you wanted it to open, it would."

"Can you tell me how to get in? Please," I added.

One word at a time they bounced a phrase around the door, each fairy twirling as it hummed its part in their reply.

"There's" "two" "ways" "to" "open."
"Though" "neither" "have" "you" "tried."
"One" "of" "them" "is" "broken."
"It's" "opposite" "force" "applied."

A riddle. My head hurt too badly for a riddle.

"Okay, say it again," I hadn't caught the whole thing.

"No way!" "Too bad!"

"Okay, okay. Something about two ways to open the door and one of them being broken."

"It's opposite force applied," Brun-Brun repeated for me.

"So the two things are opposites. Push." The fairies twittered, and I put my hand on the door, feeling their vibrations. "Christ. You need a better riddle."

"Hey!" they sang in harmony.

I shoved the door open and entered the queen's chamber. Surprisingly, the cavernous room lacked flair aside from the main attraction. The queen was sitting on a golden throne.

"Go on, get out of here!" she said, and a smiling older woman ran past me. "Honey, they should call me the Queen of Bitches.

These hags wearin' me down. Now what do *you* want?"

I positioned myself in front of the throne, looking up at the dark, curvaceous woman clad in turquoise sequins from head to toe and laughed at her question.

"I really don't have a clue. Brun-Brun told me *you* wanted to see me. I followed this guy out of Badlands, spun around a pole at the corner of Eighteenth and Castro, and apparently almost died a few minutes ago. I'm confused, and my head is pounding. So… hello there."

"You Adorable Nugget!" she said. "Aren't you sassy? Come here. Let me handle the most pressing matter. Nobody gets shit done with a hangover."

She waved her wand lazily. "*Headacus disappearus.*"

The pounding behind my temple vanished, gone completely. "Wha? How?"

"Well, the words don't do shit. I like the drama! But, enough an-tici-*pa*-tion." Her cheeks glistened as she paused. "You're the succubus boy, ain't you? Ooh, Sweetie Pie, lucky Brun-Brun's got a crush on you."

"*Succubus*? Like sex?"

"Heheh! *Succubus*. Like sex?" she repeated in a dull, flat voice. "*Succubus* got nothin' to do with sex. It's in the name." The queen put the fingernails of her right thumb and pointer finger together in front of her lips. "Drinks the soul through your… straw."

"Eh. I must be dreaming."

She cackled. "If it's a dream, dream on!"

"How did I get here? What is here?"

"You in Gairyland, Baby Boy," she said.

"Yeah, Brun-Brun tried that. But what is it?"

"Another world," she said, waving her wand in a figure eight. "One where everything is much... more... *fabulous*!" We looked at each other in awkward silence before she waved her wand again. This time it spat out a puff of glitter, and she laughed. "Woo! *This* is where you come from. It's where all the gays come from, in spirit at least."

"Sure. You're the Queen of Witches, but my parents are Wendy and Marco. I'm Sam DeSalvo."

"I'm Sam DeSalvo," she mocked again, making me sound slower and dumber than I'd like to think I sound. "We all come from somewhere, even though we are who we are. Before I was the queen, I was Dionysia, and yet I still am."

"I don't understand."

"You're not supposed to. Haven't you always felt different? Like somethin' was different about you?"

"Yeah, but then I came out. You're all obsessed with that. Yes. I am gay."

"So you are! That's why you're here. You're gay and this is Gay Heaven. Gevin!"

"Enough with the word thing. You know you're not answering my questions." Talking to the queen was pointless. "Maybe I got drugged. Maybe I'm going to wake up in an alley or back at my house."

"Don't bet on that one, Sasquatch." She seemed preoccupied with her glitter nail clip-ons.

"It's got something to do with the pole at Castro and Eighteenth. Brun-Brun said, 'The pole doesn't spin for anyone.' What did he mean?"

"This world is hidden from the one you came from, the one you think of as the *real world*. Though, that's a matter of perspective. What B's talkin' about's a phrase around here. You know... 'that way,' 'a bit funny,' 'on the bus,' 'friend of Dorothy.'"

"Jesus, of course. That's been established."

"So, you found us! Sucker may have dragged you here, but why not join us?"

"Join you in what... some cult?"

Queen opened her arms. "You could stay, Loverboy! Or,"—she refolded them—"you could bounce back and forth for a while if you've got ties back home. Whatever you want. As Queen of Witches, I invite you to stay." Her invitation merited some type of response, but I couldn't pin it down. "Don't make me wave my wand again."

"Uh."

"Brun-Brun!" she yelled, and my escort entered her chamber. "Show Sam DeSalvo around. When he's ready, be a darling and take him to the Spectrum."

"Of course." He bowed and motioned for me to come with him back through the gemstone door.

"Do whatever you want, Pumpkin Spice. This place is all about doin' as you please. Now"—she sat upright—"farewell, bitches. Queeny's takin' a break!"

A lazy twirl of her wand sent an ostentatious stream of glitter in my direction. Unsure if a thanks, a bow, or a fuck-you was needed, I stuck with silence until we were back outside her chamber.

"I think I want to go back," I said.

"Already? Aren't you even curious?"

"I'm confused, and the queen didn't quite convince me this isn't a dream."

Brun-Brun nodded. "Sooo."

"Ugh. Fine! Dream on!"

Chapter 16

Out of the Closet

The night before the queen's meeting with the Global Rights Organization, I did what I did most nights—search for Brun-Brun. By retracing what he'd shown me after leaving the queen's chamber that first time, I hoped I'd find him—or at least some trace. Hell, I'd ask the succubus if I saw him!

"Hey!" Adele's voice startled me.

I turned back to look at my friend jogging out of the Ivory Tower's front gate.

"Can I join?" she asked. "On the hunt, I assume? My lips are sealed." She zipped them. "*I* want the company. So, I promise not to badger you for wandering the streets alone, late at night, searching for your long-lost love."

"Off to a great start. Come on, we're starting at Pansy's. You can grab an Orgie. Looks like you need it."

Walking down Main Street, I remembered feeling like this

was the underbelly of San Francisco. Back then I saw myself as beneath the Castro, upside down on its mirror image. Brun-Brun had corrected me over a pint in Pansy's Pub-erty. It isn't just the Castro; this world is connected to every gayborhood on Earth.

"You gonna have one too?" Adele asked, turning to the bar.

"We're retracing my first day here," I said. "This is where Brun-Brun gave me my first drink. It wouldn't be a thorough search if I didn't!"

Remembering my first day in the new world was like channeling memories of a former life. Brun-Brun had described the transformation everyone here experienced; he called it the Spectrum, and he made sure I experienced it before he disappeared.

Pansy's was empty except for a few late-night drinkers at a corner of the bar. Its younger patrons were at late night haunts, leaving the grey gays to continue in peace, and by their raucous laughter I wondered if the younger kids were missing out. I grabbed a table next to the crackling hearth while Adele ordered.

"To a successful search," she proclaimed, and we clinked glasses. "So, what did you and this dream man talk about on your first day?"

"Orgie. Brun-Brun sat right where you are, waiting to laugh as I took my first sip."

I tilted the glass to my lips, recreating the moment, feeling the cool pink fog rush into my nostrils before the purple liquid hit my mouth. Its sweetness I expected, but the flood of sensations—minty warmth, an electric buzz, and tingling pleasure pumped to every extremity—would always surprise.

"I remember my first." Adele lifted her eyebrows. "Got me comin' back for more, that's for sure."

I closed my eyes to enjoy the Orgie washing over me.

"I moaned the first time." I imagined Brun-Brun's mischievous smirk across from me and repeated what he'd told me. "For men, women, and the undecided. You never get used to it, but you do learn to quiet down."

"Miracle," Adele said. "Orgasm, full night's sleep, plus it comes in juice boxes!"

I took another sip and let the electricity seize my muscles. The voyeuristic, instant ecstasy was addictive.

"You must really miss him," Adele said.

"Kind of a loaded question. Like I'm a huge creeper. We didn't know each other that long before he disappeared."

"Yeah. You're weird." She laughed. "But I know there's something else."

"Short version is that a succubus lured me here, and Brun-Brun saved me. All that was before I knew about the Spectrum or my wonderful status as a Blank Canvas."

"That Blank Canvas thing's a head scratcher. Any progress learning a power?" I rolled my eyes. "It'll happen. Hell, if the queen really is one too you've got a lot to look forward to. At least you got closet travel."

If the queen was a Blank Canvas than I was in danger, but every member of the Scales of Justice was in too deep. I didn't want to burden her with my feeling of being on constant guard; so I deflected.

"There's two of us here. What's your excuse for being out at four in the morning?"

"I need another if we're getting into this." She chugged her Orgie, and I slid mine across the table as compensation. "It's my ex. Not just an ex, like several ex's ago. The original ex. We met in high school. Well, I was in high school. She was in college. Proud and properly angry, she was happy to teach a new lesbian the wonders of feminism."

"And scissoring?" I prodded.

Adele flipped me off. "It was stupid. I was stupid!"

"Who isn't their first time around?"

"I had a full ride to any public college in Berlin. Turned them all down to go be with her in Cologne."

"Yeah that's kind of stupid," I said.

"I showed up on her doorstep… as a surprise."

"Holy shit!" I couldn't contain my smile. "You didn't tell her?"

"We were seeing each other! I was in love! She said so too. I mean who wouldn't want their long distance girlfriend on their doorstep?"

"Oh Adele. Nobody wants that. Please tell me she wasn't with someone else? Did you walk in on them?"

"Ugh. Less drama, more embarrassment. She was great, but when she opened the door and I yelled '*surprise*,' I knew I'd made a mistake. Her face dropped. So, I did what any self-respecting homeless, jobless, broken-hearted girl would do: I faked it. Mooching was not what I'd imagined during my six hour drive to Cologne, but I pretended not to notice the obvious, dreading she'd ask me to leave before I could figure shit out."

"Did you?"

"I'm here aren't I?"

I laughed. "That was ages ago. What happened tonight?"

"I kissed her."

"Wait... she's here?"

"I knew she was here." Adele was bright red, half hiding behind her pint. "I swear I thought I was over her, but we were at the party, got to talking, she leaned forward and...."

"You kissed. So what?"

"She was picking up an earring. I thought she—. I mean, she leaned—. Ahh! I assaulted her face! She jumped back, picked up her hoop, and made this ridiculous face, like *just my hoop!*"

Now, I was challenging the bar's laughter with my own. "What happened?"

"I apologized! She apologized! Oh it was awful. She re-explained that we were over. I know we're over. I'm over it! I thought she—ugh."

"You do need another drink," I said.

"Is it that bad? I mean—."

"No. It's that bad."

She hopped out of her chair. "Can we please walk? I need to move. I'm losing it!"

"This makes me feel way better about my search for Brun-Brun. At least we can lose it together."

"Let's just go, please," she said.

"Alright alright. But first, can you grab my napkin? I dropped it, and I don't want to send mixed signals... ha!"

"Say something again. Come on. I dare you." Her glare reminded me of her Spectrum ability. "Where are we off to next?"

"Transpo Hub Square."

We took Main Street away from the Ivory Tower. Even with a clear sky, it was impossible to see the top of the tower. That first day, a tower that went up forever was incomprehensible. It still didn't make sense, but nothing on my list of impossibilities was worth pondering.

The main drag was filled with quirky storefronts that made sense in a world where the Spectrum existed. Apothecaries, weapon shops that looked like sex shops, and sex shops that looked like weapon shops. We passed one window showcasing something that could have been either—an imprisonment cock ring that turned its wearer into a slave.

"Do you think you're going to bump into him while checking out cock rings at four thirty in the morning?" Adele asked. "Like, 'Hey, Sam! Gosh, long time no see!'"

"We can always go back to talking about how much you love your ex," I replied

"What? That's a fair question! I'm enhancing your search, not making fun."

"I'm hoping I know when I find it." I considered leaving it there. "Helps me stay sane in the meantime. Time to process the shitstorm we live every day."

"Sometimes I wonder if processing's the wrong thing to do."

Transpo Hub Square lay in the center of the city, with three sides bounded by skinny buildings, two to three windows across and three or four stories tall. Each one rested against its neighbors, barely askew, creating a quaint but disorienting feeling that the whole city was slightly unstable. The Transpo Hub itself stood about twice as tall as the other buildings and made up an entire side of the square.

The sidewalk split, parting around a grassy hill in the middle of the square where a bronze statue of an open door stood prominently. I ran up the hill. The bronzed statue at its peak was twice the size of any closet door in the hub, and it framed the Transpo Hub's concrete arch entry. Two giggling guys stumbled beneath the arch, their flirting echoing across the empty square and down an alley, leaving the square in a rare state of calm.

"Two drunks," Adele said. "That what you're after?"

I stepped through the bronze statue and read the inscription on the side facing the Transpo Hub, *Come out and see the new world.*

"Wonder if whoever made this knew how true it would be right now?"

"Maybe not the war, but the struggle's always been there. It's always been true."

We walked down the other side of the hill, beneath the arch, and into the Transpo Hub's open-air, main chamber. There was no machinery, no beeping, nor electronics of any kind. Inside, there was nothing but doors.

Every gayborhood in the world, all connected to this place by closet doors. Velvet ropes ran through the room, creating small empty spaces in front of each door. A city name was inscribed above each one. Some of them were familiar: Barrio Norte, Beaubourg, Collingwood, Darlinghurst, Farme de Amoedo….

Natural portals were natural connections between the two worlds available to those who know where to look. Most were unknown, but they were the singular means of travel between worlds until the Spectrum test. The Spectrum unlocked travel by closet door, and the Transpo Hub was the network center. It was too late for the laughter, shouting, and hugging that usually filled the place.

"Feels more like an airport terminal than a rip in space-time," I said. "Transplants like us think these doors lead home. Everyone else thinks they lead to a vacation spot."

"Don't see the queen calling the other side of these doors home," Adele said. "Sounds like she had it pretty rough. You think this is revenge?"

"I don't know. Did Willy Wonka do all that stuff to the kids out of revenge?" I bobbed up and down, smiling.

"What?" she asked. "What are you doing?"

"Oompa Loompa, doopa-dee-do."

Laughing, we strolled the aisles of closet doors. Each was unique, but remarkably similar considering they led to locations I'd once considered the whole world—cities, continents, hemispheres, side by side in neat rows and columns. A light beam cut across our path as one of the doors opened, a white heel and dress entering the Transpo Hub from the other side—my world—with a little girl following after. Someone blocked our path and our view of whoever had stepped out of the door.

"Halt!" he shouted.

Adele ignited both arms. "Out of our way, punk."

She could defend us. Her Spectrum results had revealed that she could control fire.

"Flamer." The man recognized her power. "You need to leave."

The figure he protected closed the door carefully before taking the hand of the little girl and turning toward us.

Adele increased the throughput of her radiating flames. "It's a free world, and we'll damn well go where we want. Back off."

The guard pulled a strand of beads taut between his gloved

hands. This was going to go much worse for me than anyone else. The Spectrum had told me I was a Blank Canvas, which so far hadn't meant a thing. I was completely defenseless.

"Wait!" Only one person would be sneaking out of the Transpo Hub under the cover of personal guards, and I shouted her name. "Enyo!"

The obscured figure reached her guard and placed a white glove on his shoulder.

"You," said the woman in white. "What do *you* want?"

"I'm looking for Brun-Brun. I've been looking for you too. I think something may have hap—." I cut myself off, remembering Adele was on edge beside me.

"You know these people?" Adele asked.

"Sort of. They're friends of Brun-Brun's."

"Not friends of yours," Enyo said. "Why shouldn't I have you killed?"

Adele cast a fiery column that almost reached the Transpo Hub ceiling.

"Like to see you try," she said. "Why don't you go that way, and we'll go this way?"

"Adele," Enyo said. "With two members of the Scales of Justice before me, there's only one way."

"Stop," I pleaded. "I'm telling you I think you may have been right."

"Of course I'm right!" Enyo's lip flared. "Look at what's happened. Can't you see that your queen is nothing but a misguided boy lashing out? I'm the only one who can make this right, and nothing will get in my way."

I looked around the empty Transpo Hub, realizing Enyo was

the person least likely to help me. I was everything she hated. Worse. I'd chosen it.

"Sam, what the hell is going on?" Adele begged.

"This is Enyo, the queen's sister." I wanted to apologize.

"Sure, and I'm the queen's nephew."

As she said *phew* she jumped up and replanted her feet, one in front of the other. Pointing ahead, she released a torrent of fire, drawing sweat from my forehead as the heat from her attack intensified. Her flames parted right, revealing Enyo's unscathed guard right where he'd been standing.

"Shit! A Fieldmaker!" Adele shouted. "RUN!"

The guard twirled the beads like nunchucks, and an invisible field lifted us off the ground. We hurtled up toward the ceiling too fast to think about finding the unseeable edge before we were already too high to jump.

"I'm sorry!" I said. "It's all—"

Adele shoved me off the rising field and jumped off after me. A howl accompanied our approaching death, and a brown blur galloped down the closet-lined path below.

"Get Sam!" Adele shouted, blasting a column of fire at Enyo as she fell.

The blur leaped impossibly high, colliding with my body and crushing me with a familiar hug. We hit the ground hard, and my friend whimpered as something shattered. He didn't let go, cradling me like an egg-drop contraption, built to break in specific places. When we stopped rolling, I lifted his bulky arms off me.

"Benj!" I put my hand on his wolf-form and met his cloudy eyes. He took shallow breaths to keep from moving. "You'll be okay. Thank you. You saved my life."

"Ha!" Enyo walked the aisle toward us, guard at her side, still holding the little girl's hand.

"SAM!" Adele shouted from across the Transpo Hub, too far away to help in time.

"I was looking for Brun-Brun!" I cried. "I was trying to make things right!"

"Make things right?!" Enyo mocked. "You keep making things worse."

"I'm trying!" I begged. "Please! Don't hurt my friends."

"Find Brun-Brun," she said.

Enyo extended the hand not already holding the little girl's, and the Fieldmaker took it. The three of them disappeared.

"SAM!" Adele was running toward us. "Are you okay? Where did they go?"

"Benj is hurt," I said.

"What the fuck, Sam? How do you know those people?" Adele asked.

"I'm sorry! This is bad."

Benj's body slowly transformed back into his bulging human form.

"Benj! Are you okay? Don't move," Adele said, but Benj forced himself to stand, cradling his arm.

"Sam," he said. "We're yer friends. What was that?"

"She was telling the truth. She's the queen's sister. Brun-Brun introduced me after getting my Spectrum results."

Chapter 3

The Spectrum

"You'll be fine," said Brun-Brun.

"But I still don't understand."

"I can't really explain it. The Spectrum was created to learn about you and, through that knowledge, awaken your ability. I'm a Sentry. Working for the queen is my job, but Sentry is my Spectrum designation. The Spectrum unlocks these abilities. It's the easiest way for Transplants like you to get acquainted with our world. The Spectrum'll tell you about you. What you do with those results—even ignoring them—is up to you."

"I could be a succubus… or a witch?"

"It's easier to explain once you've done it, but you could be anything. The Spectrum also lets you use the closets to travel back and forth."

He seemed eager. I was too. A test to unlock a magic power promised to fulfill all my YA series fantasies.

"Okay. Wish me luck!"

Brun-Brun leaned in, and the door flew open.

"You must be Sam!" boomed a beaming, colossal man.

Blushing, Brun-Brun turned to leave.

"What? Ahh. Sorry for the cock block there, buddy. Hya hya!" The giant man slapped me hard on my back, propelling me through the door before he closed it. "I'm Benj, Spectrum proctor by day."

Benj was at least three times my size. Everything about him was massive: giant biceps, bushy sideburns, thick, muscular legs. Everything except his pants. They seemed almost spray-painted onto his oversized bottom half, leaving very little to the imagination.

"Hey. I'm Sam, like you said."

Not exactly Professor X. I looked desperately for the situation room. No mad scientist laboratory. The circular room looked like a classroom with a single desk at its center.

"No need for small talk. Most folks prefer gettin' on with it. I'll know you real good after this anyway! Hya hya!"

I tried to laugh. "Yeah, I guess."

"Not prescriptive... descriptive. Answer the questions, and the Spectrum'll give a recommendation, yer Spectrum Guide. Contains all the different paths you can learn. Course, you can do whatever you want, but I've never seen anyone succeed in learnin' anythin' past page ten."

I looked back at the door where Brun-Brun had left me, half bothering to understand what the gigantic man said as he dropped his foot up on the desk.

"Notice anythin' strange about me?" he asked.

I looked at the giant, hairy man leaning against his knee, his crotch uncomfortably close to my face, and desperately tried to think of an inoffensive response. He was what I'd call a bear, noticeably handsome, but there was more to it than his preference for drinks at 440 Castro over Toad Hall. He seemed to be an actual bear, or—

"Werewolf. See?" A few strands of his beard grew longer, his ears became pointed, and his jaw elongated before it all reversed and his cheeks flushed. "You should see yer face."

"Uh. I'm— Sorry. It's—."

He laughed. "Don't worry. Spectrum virgins all react the same. Pretty hard to believe."

"How is this possible?" I said.

"The Spectrum learns about you. The Spectrum Guide takes all that info and suggests abilities that might be buried inside ya."

"Inside me." I thought about that. "And one of those might be becoming a werewolf?"

"Was for me." I couldn't help but laugh. This was ridiculous. "Real kicker's how you learn yer ability. Ain't nothin' to it. Sure, you can try to be a basketball player, but most people don't got it in 'em no matter how much they practice. The test helps rule out all the stuff yer not cut out for."

The door opened, and I looked over, hoping to see Brun-Brun. Benj stood up taller and bowed a little.

"Ma'am!"

"Like a priest in a brothel—everything's a possibility!" The queen waved, twinkling her fingers. "Oh, calm down, Benj. Just dropping in for a little check-in with our newest guest."

"Yes, Ma'am." He nodded to me, and her heels clicked a few feet closer.

"Isn't it fabulous?" she asked. "I'm sure you don't believe it, of course, but that's half the fun, being swept up in it all. I mean, who wouldn't *want* to believe?"

I suddenly felt awkward. Benj was still on edge.

"I don't get it. How does it work?" I said.

"Oh, it's boring. Psychology, physiology, homology, and a bunch of other… *shit*. Doesn't matter. You get five little scores and a personal guide to—*possibility*!"

"It's genius," Benj said with a smile.

"It's what you do with your guide that matters. Hammers don't sculpt." She winked. "Good luck, Sam. After this, everything will change."

"Brun-Brun said that. But, uhh. Thanks."

"Toodles!" She left through the same door, and Benj finally relaxed.

"This place is too much," I said.

"Personal visit from the queen?!"

"Yeah. That should be exciting?"

Benj nodded, either confirming excitement or confounded that I wasn't. He opened the only other door in the circular room.

"Take a peek," he said. "This is where I'll be while you take it. All by my lonesome in the tiny waiting room. You ready?"

"Does anyone ever say yes?" I asked.

"Hya hya! I don't think anyone's ever meant it! Test is already on yer desk. Take as much time as you want." He grabbed my arm with his thumb and pointer finger. "We start now. Go on!"

He gave me a small shove back into the circular room and shut the door between us.

"Huh. O-kay."

The door to Benj's waiting area was before me, with the exit door next to it. The rest of the room was plain: wood floor, soft white paint on the walls, and in the middle, a piece of paper and a pencil on a desk. It had to be a practical joke, but I'd seen the Transpo Hub. The closet doors would open if I did this one thing. So, I sat down and flipped over the paper.

The Paper Test

Welcome to the Paper Test. You will be recorded and you will be timed. There are no grades or correct answers.

I. Do anything with this test.
II. Answer, or do not answer, the questions.
III. Take as much time as you'd like.

#1 The egg
A. Came before the chicken
B. Eats iguanas
C. None of the above

#2 Would you prefer to call yourself
A. A piece of cardboard
B. A straw wrapper
C. None of the above

#3 You are almost never late for
A. A date
B. A funeral
C. None of the above

#4 You feel at ease
A. In a crowd by yourself
B. By yourself in a crowd
C. None of the above

#5 You are
A. Shy and participatory
B. Rowdy and quiet
C. None of the above

#6 You believe in
A. An afterlife
B. A panda bear
C. None of the above

#7 Your best friend calls you
A. Pragmatically challenged
B. Visionary-ly challenged
C. None of the above

#8 Money is
A. The root of all evil
B. A necessary evil
C. None of the above

#9 Murder is
A. The root of all evil
B. A necessary evil
C. None of the above

#10 Open relationships
A. Highway
B. Cabin
C. None of the above

I should have expected absurdity, but somehow I had convinced myself these questions might identify my personality, like the Myers-Briggs of Gairyland. I looked at the room's two doors, then at the solid walls, waiting for someone to announce I'd been punk'd. There didn't seem to be anything recording me. This wasn't an interrogation room. There was no one-way mirror to Benj's room, just him, waiting patiently in a tiny adjacent space.

Divergent had serums and hallucinations and fights for true identity. If I was dreaming, was this piece of paper all my imagination could muster?

One final scan of the paper confirmed my answers were 100 percent incapable of doing anything the Spectrum had promised. So, I promptly marked ten random answers— A-C-A-A-C-B-C-A-C-C —and knocked on Benj's door.

"Whoa! All ready? Okay! We got a fast one!" he said to no one. "Hya hya!"

"Have you seen the test?"

"Hyeah! Not very high on the Boundlessy chart." Benj put

his hulking arm over my shoulder, adding about twenty pounds to my walk into the tiny observation room.

"What does that mean?"

"Didn't you see the instructions? Answerin' a question at all's like an infinite amount of decisions. Bet you put one answer for each, didn't you?"

I'd missed the whole point. It was all one think-outside-the-box test.

"The questions didn't matter at all, did they?" I said.

"'Course they matter. Everythin' matters. You'll see. Somehow. The Spectrum gets it right, every time. Come on. Through here."

He pushed me toward the back wall of the tiny observation room and gave me a powerful shove. I fell through the wall. There was no chill or feeling at all as I passed into the true observation room filled with wires, stacks of processors, TV monitors, metallic flasks, a Bunsen burner, and dripping liquids.

"What is all this?" I asked.

"Sorry! Had to keep this part hidden. The belly of the beast. All this is the Spectrum."

It took both his hands to peel open his pocket, and after some digging, he slid a tiny black remote out from where it had glued itself to his thigh.

"Wshoo. Not made for werewolves." His face was bright red. "First, congratulations! Completin' the Spectrum starts yer journey to unlockin' yer true ability!"

He clicked a button on the remote, and one of the monitors came to life. Projected onto it was a live feed of the testing room. The monitor showed a recording of me cautiously approaching the desk before flipping over the ten-question test.

"Recordin' done here's a bit more than you prob'ly imagined." He clicked another button, and the monitor filled with an overlay of information. Benj pointed to a line graph floating next to my head. "Heart rate monitor. Blink counter. Pupil size. We're measuring CO_2, O_2, H_2O, argon, nitrogen… that's just when ya breath. The Spectrum measures it *all*."

He paused to give me a big cheesy grin, then kept going. This was a speech he'd given many times, and loved it.

"There are cameras, and sensors, and thingamajigs everywhere. Let's see…"

He pointed at different graphs plastered on top of the recorded video that blinked between perspectives of me sitting at the desk, looking confused.

"Here's the data we get from the pencil. Grip strength, moisture level, writin' pressure, holdin' angle, all that."

"How is this possible?"

"Hya hya! This! I turned into a werewolf, Sam."

He clicked the remote again, and the recording was replaced by a lopsided star inscribed inside a pentagon.

"There we have it! Yer results. To put it real creepy… *you*. Together, the five Spectrum attributes make up somethin' like yer fingerprint. And look at that! Not so low on Boundlessy after all. Tells you how much I know!"

He gave me a chummy push, which almost knocked me down.

"The pentagram's five points represent a hundred percent for each Spectrum attribute. The points of yer star-shaped thing represent how much of each attribute you've got. Closer to the pentagram edge, means you've got more of that attribute. So, that little nub of a leg in the top left means you've got a smidge of Independitivity."

"That's not a real word, though," I said, trying to hold onto any sense of *real*.

Benj didn't respond. Instead, he pointed to the top of the pentagram and guided me through each of the five made-up personality traits bearing minor semblance to real words, caked in this place's typical flair.

"This'll make more sense when we look at yer Spectrum Guide," he assured me. "This is the fun part!"

I didn't know what to say. This was all so random, but somehow not. Like hearing my fortune with too many details for it to be a scam. Benj walked over to a printer, which had been working the whole time.

"So, you pick yer ability, and then you unlock it," he said, like *easy as that!*

"How?"

"Most folks pick whatever's first in their guide. It should be the best match. So, it'll come most naturally, but you can do whatever you want. The Spectrum provides the info, but you decide who you wanna to be."

"So, what do I do once I've decided?" I asked.

"That's the kicker." The printer stopped, and he picked up whatever it had created, holding it behind his back. "Once you've decided, yer mostly on yer own. No ceremony, no queen's blessing, no mumbo jumbo. You *believe* and *decide*."

"What does that mean?"

"Decidin' what you want and believin' it's possible are most important to gettin' what you want. Then you make it happen."

"Believe and decide…" I said to myself.

"Cryptic, but it works. Some of the test proctors use meditation exercises, yoga… few even tried inducin' abilities with Orgie 'til they found out it created dependency. I stick with believin' in you."

"And that's it," I said.

"Might come easy for you. The Ivory Tower greased my gears. Bein' surrounded by all this absurdity makes you realize anythin's possible."

He revealed the printed object behind his back: a thin book bound in a dark brown cover. There were no words printed on it. I tried to look at the printer behind Benj, but I realized it didn't matter how this book had come to be. Inside was a magic power I could learn, something that would change my life. He held it out to me.

"Wanna see yer top ability?" Benj's excitement was contagious.

"Hell yes!" I cheered. "Let's see it!"

Benj opened the cover. There on the first page was a silhouette of an androgynous human examining a canvas like a mirror. As I scanned for some clue as to what it meant, the largest words stood out. *BLANK CANVAS*.

Benj cleared his throat before reacting at all, and I read the smaller words beneath the picture. *It is all at your fingertips.*

"What does that mean?" I tried to take the book from him, but his grip was firm, turning my excitement to sudden worry. "What is Blank Canvas?"

"Oh, the queen'll wanna hear this." He looked at me, smiling. "You can do anything. Sky's the limit!"

Chapter 17

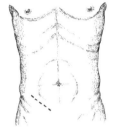

Global Rights Organization

"It's a threat," I said.

Benj picked up the letter I'd found slipped under my door, and as he read, sparkling flakes fell off its glitter-penned words.

"*Heard about last night. Sorry my sister's cray. Best not leave the tower 'til I'm back. We need to talk. For your own good.*" Benj looked at Adele for reassurance. "What about that's a threat?"

Adele grabbed the note. "Let's say everything you've told us is true," she said. "That the queen is kidnapping people for some reason. That she isn't just fighting for equality. That there's a crazier plan and her sister is trying to stop her from destroying a whole world."

"Don't forget," Benj said, "the nugget that all this requires Sam's help. No offense, but bein' a Blank Canvas doesn't seem all it's cracked up to be. Yer not exactly a war asset."

Adele kept trying my story, even as it became more ludicrous.

"Sam mentioned that Enyo knows the queen is also a Blank Canvas. If Sam could be capable of even a fraction of what the queen can do, he'd make a powerful ally... or enemy."

"So why not kill 'em?" Benj asked. "Sorry, this isn't makin' sens—"

"Stop," I interrupted. "This is why I hadn't told anyone. I didn't want you involved, because I don't know what to believe either."

"We're involved I'd say!" Benj rubbed his healing arm. "We got a job to do. The Scales exist to check and balance against this. We wouldn't approve a plan that didn't do more good than harm. I know you didn't agree with Love Crimes, but it's a long way from destroyin' a whole world. Yer part of that. Don't throw it all away over one disagreement. And sure as hell don't do it over some conspiracy theory."

"Please, don't say anything to the queen," I said. "I've already got to deal with whatever this note means when she gets back."

"Yer tellin' me you don't want us to tell the queen about yer secret plot against her?" Benj seemed betrayed. "She *trusts* you!"

"*This*"—I held up the glitter note—"doesn't convey trust. Let the queen and I handle our shit."

"Fine." Benj wanted the conversation to end.

I wasn't swayed. The queen was involved somehow in Brun-Brun's disappearance, in all of them. She'd looked past my meeting with her sister, but there was no way she'd ignore this. I was in danger, and I didn't want her suspecting the whole Scales of plotting against her. We'd managed to force a meeting with the Global Rights Organization, and this could ruin it. As Benj walked away and Adele looked at me trying to understand my perspective, there was tension. Not tension—distrust—and that's how we entered the control room to watch the queen represent Renegayd.

*****

"Thanks, Hun, for agreeing to meet."

Apollo Vazquez, leader of the Global Rights Organization, sat next to the queen, who put out her hand as she thanked him.

"Love your outfit," he said, taking her hand.

Mentioning the outlandish scene made his apparent discomfort less awkward. Apollo was reserved in stature and personality, further dwarfed by the queen's feathery outfit, which stretched up and out of view of the camera.

"Why, thank you! And you are looking quite… comfortable."

He smiled, and their hands split, each moving to the armrest of their leather seat.

"I'm not used to making quite such a scene of everything I do," he replied. "Something Renegayd's made a habit. I can see the influence."

"Thank ya, Sweetie. Pleasantries out the way. Let's cut straight to it then. Shall we?" Apollo nodded, allowing the queen to move first. "How about you tell me what you love most about this world."

Apollo's brow furrowed, and he shifted in his chair.

"Excuse me?" he said.

"We're here because we have different methods of achieving the same thing. I come from a place where we already have that thing: liberation… Perfect Equality. That's what I love most about my world. I want to know what you love most about this one."

Apollo was still, thinking hard or looking like it, before speaking. "I'd have to say its diversity. Different people, different places, different opinions—it makes the humanity binding us together more potent, deeper than if we were all the same."

"Much deeper... About six feet under some times." Her grin was wide, sinister.

"You think our differences are killing us?" Apollo said.

"I think you're playing a trick. Diversity invokes race, creed, religion, political party, haircut! I'm talking about sexuality. Your favorite part of your world is the differences in sexuality? That's ridiculous."

"It's ridiculous to purport genocide against people with a different opinion. It's ridiculous to suggest killing everyone with a different point of view."

The queen did what she does best, poke and enjoying the reaction.

"Two thousand seven," she said. "You must have cheered when the USA's Employment Non-Discrimination Act had transgender protections removed to get it passed. Yet another sacrifice for the needs of the ignorant."

"No one celebrated that change," Apollo said. "We celebrated a historic victory for our community—even if that victory was imperfect."

"And how many trans people were harmed by your tempered celebration, rather than militant unrest? When your rights have been taken, you don't reap new progress, you reclaim innate dignity, and it can happen all at once. Renegayd is making it happen, and that's not ridiculous. The opposite point of view causes harm, so we're stomping it out as fast as we can. And

Baby, we are fast. Remember when your parents caught you with a porn magazine?" Apollo blushed as the queen continued. "That night you thought about killing yourself. That night was hard. That night was harm. And many don't make it to the day."

He took a deep breath. "I'm not sure what you hope to accomplish by publicizing my childhood."

"There is a right and a wrong on this issue. Can we agree on that?"

"We can't agree on anything," Apollo said.

"So, for you, homophobia—and all its physical and mental abuse—is a legitimate opinion?" Spotting her trap, Apollo remained calm and silent until she continued. "Got your appendix?"

"You're not helping your cause by broadcasting this." The queen remained silent, blinking once to show she'd wait until he answered. "Yes, I still have my appendix. No reason to get rid of it."

"No reason to get rid of it," she repeated. "You know, one in fifteen people will get appendicitis. Some will die, and some will just hurt."

"Homosexuality is not like appendicitis, if that's what you're suggesting."

"Not queers. Hate! It's the hate that's hurting us. Renegayd's ripping out a ticking time bomb! Nobody misses something that's solitary use is potential harm."

"These are people we're talking about!" Apollo showed his first burst of emotion. "Killing a human being is not analogous to removing an appendix. We need change without violence."

"Only a philosophy of eternity could justify nonviolence. You see, people don't live forever; so, lollygagging comes at the cost of LGBT lives. We suffer for the convenience of our oppressor."

And then there was an explosion. Shǎng's scream jolted me out of my seat as Dionysia and Apollo disappeared in a blinding flash. Gunfire filled the airwaves, and the Scales of Justice, along with the whole world, was on edge until the camera refocused. When it did, the scene had changed. Three Mission Morality members surrounded Apollo and the queen, who were still seated at the center of the camera shot.

"You disgust me," said the man holding his gun inches from the queen. "Everything that's wrong with this world."

"This is not the way to deal with your frustration," Apollo offered. "What do you want?"

His question got the gun shoved in his face.

"To eliminate the vermin, but you just keep spreadin'. So, we'll kill the queen to destroy the hive."

"Oh, Sweetpea, you know bees aren't vermin," the queen said.

"Shut it!"

"Kill her!" another said.

"That thing still on? I want them to see it."

The queen stood up, and the men's anger turned to fear. They panicked, shouting, and throwing their weapons to the ground.

"You'll wanna hold onto those," she said, picking up a gun, which had transformed into a dildo.

The three men doubled over, screaming. Blood dripped from their crotches.

Adele put her hand on my shoulder. "Holy—"

"Shit!" Benj shouted. "She blew up their dicks!"

Hearing the groans and seeing the men with their hands clamped between their legs made it seem possible—probable knowing the queen.

"No need to thank me, Apollo. Simple appen-*dick*-tomy." She pointed her wand lazily at Apollo. "I think you're right. We don't agree on much. Lucky for you, Renegayd is going to keep working on your behalf—no agreement necessary."

The queen examined the silicone shaft, which seconds ago had threatened her life. I thought she might deep throat it for show, but instead, she blew air across the top as if she'd fired it.

"Let me tell you what's going to happen." She pointed the dildo at the camera. "The LGBT community will have liberation. There will be no middle ground. There will be no impartiality. We will have no mercy on our enemies. This is the end of indifference. You're either with us, or we blow your balls off. Don't got any?"

A halfhearted jab of her wand made history as—in perfect camera focus—the middle and ring finger on Apollo's outstretched hand melted. New skin grew from his knuckles, wrapping around both fingers that now drooped above his wrist, while the transformation continued. The world stared with Apollo, horrified, at a new set of balls jiggling in front of his face, right between his pointer and pinky fingers.

The queen stepped in front of the camera, blocking the leader of the Global Rights Organization with her feathery silhouette.

"Renegayd needs you to grow a pair."

Chapter 4

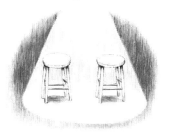

Enyo

I clutched my new Spectrum Guide as the elevator climbed higher in the Ivory Tower.

"Got you a room on B26. Stay as long as you like." Macy Freid was short, but she worked all four-feet-something with a gorgeous, ruby-red dress. She tapped her heel, and I realized about six inches of her four feet was stiletto. She had to look straight up for our eyes to meet. "I'm sorry. But, I'm dying to know what you'll pick first!"

"What do you mean?"

"Blank Canvas! I heard your guide was filled with every possibility. My Spectrum Guide had five pages, five possibilities, but like everyone else I couldn't manage to learn beyond page one: The Stage."

As she said the name of her Spectrum ability, the elevator lights became spotlights. Her movement, even confined to the ascending lift, enchanted, and she performed:

"The Spectrum omits what you can't achieve,
But beyond page three you'll find is naïve.
Something you're not, the fantasies deceive.
Stay true to yourself, to find your reprieve."

I opened my Spectrum Guide, and Macy hurried over, her spotlight illuminating the first page of my guide: Blank Canvas. I flipped to page two, which was empty, and the next, and the next. The whole book was blank except for the first page.

"The plot thickens!" Macy shouted, and then clapped, deactivating her Stage power.

"My one choice is some vague suggestion of every choice… what does that mean?" I held back a laugh and a cry.

"Who knows, Blanks Canvas," she said. "I wouldn't have guessed it from the look of you. No offense. I mean you look normal." She bumbled as the elevator ascended. "I mean like a nice everyman. Or something."

"Umm… thanks?"

The elevator ding bailed Macy out, and she hurried into a white hallway. In the florescent light, Macy's dress cast a brilliant shadow on the empty hall's white tiles. She swung her hips as she led us past several doors marked with room numbers.

"Where is everyone?"

"Not much goin' on here except for sleeping. During the day most people go out and live life." Macy stopped in front of one of the doors. "314. Got that? B26, room 314. Retina scanner is programmed to you and you alone." Macy extended her hand, and I took it. "It's really exciting to meet you. Can't wait to see what you can do for us."

"Me too," I faked.

Macy's heels clicked back toward the elevator. I was more excited to be alone—to process for a minute everything that had happened. There was a quick, bright flash from a sensor in the middle of the door, and then my room swung open. Inside was nothing like the hallway. The tiny entryway had dark green carpet and a picture of the *Wizard of Oz* movie cover. Dorothy, Wizard, Lion, Tin Man, and Scarecrow—the whole gang welcomed me to my room. How appropriate.

"Hey, Sam."

I nearly jumped out of my skin as Brun-Brun came around the corner.

"What are you doing?" I asked.

"Sorry! Geez, you should have seen yourself."

"I just learned that my room opens for me and me alone."

Brun-Brun gave me a hug, ending my desire to be alone. The familiar face was better.

"You okay?" he asked.

"I don't know. It's overwhelming."

I threw my Spectrum Guide onto a table at the foot of the bed, and Brun-Brun grabbed my hand.

"Blank Canvas," he said. "I know."

"Seems like everyone does. What's it mean?"

He squeezed me before letting go to run his hands through his hair. Whatever it meant was taxing for Brun-Brun to think about.

"I don't know. Look, Sam, I'm sorry, but if you're confused now it's about to get a whole lot worse."

"I think I'm developing a coping resistance to confusion," I said. "What's up now?"

"I brought you to the queen because I had to. She knew the minute you crossed over that a Transplant had come through the portal. She looks for people like you—outsiders." He looked around the room before whispering, "She's building an army."

Brun-Brun wasn't only a familiar face; he'd saved me from a soul-sucking succubus and been at my side since going through the Castro portal. Compared to Benj, Brun-Brun looked slight, but he was still much more fit than I was. His comment should have warranted a different reaction.

"Take off your pants," I said.

Brun-Brun's eyebrows furrowed—"What?"—but his cheeks gave him away.

"You heard me."

"Sam, this is serious. You're in danger. Lots of people are—"

I shoved him backward, hard. His face twisted into panic as he tripped over the foot of the bed and fell. I was on top of him when his back hit the comforter.

"Whatever," I said, and split his button-up shirt open.

When I did, a pair of wings sprung out from his sides.

"You've, uh. Got wings."

He smiled sheepishly. He was gorgeous. Normally I'd have been so shocked to have someone like him in my bed that the last thing I'd be doing is what I actually wanted, but nothing about today was normal. Wings be damned, I unbuttoned his fly to massage him through his underwear.

"Sam" was all he said.

With one hand busy, my other balled around his blond hair to force his chin upwards. I traced my tongue down from his Adam's apple. He could have thrown me off but instead gave in.

I arched forward, and the contact of our bare chests sent waves of heat across my whole body.

"Hurry," he said.

His urgency made me mad, and I curled my fingers around the waistband of his grey underwear and ripped downward. He winced at the sudden jolt that tugged his hard-on downward before releasing it.

"Don't say one more fucking word."

This is what I needed—control—and Brun-Brun obliged.

Side by side, rising and falling. There was no affection. No kissing. No caressing. Pleasure and a flash of power. Like I could fool myself by lying with a strange man, in a strange place, on a bed I'd never seen before. It was still the most familiar thing that had happened all day.

Breathing heavy, still sweating, I couldn't ignore it any longer.

"What do you mean an army?"

"I can't say. I mean, I can't explain it. Not like Enyo can."

"I'm guessing Enyo doesn't want to talk here?" I said.

Brun-Brun sat up beside me, making me feel small again with his broad shoulders and folded wings.

"We'll have to go to her," he said.

"Okay. So what? We ride an elephant-sized turtle over a rainbow? Jump into the toilet transit system and flush ourselves to her secret hideout?"

He laughed, brushing his hair away from his face to look at me.

"What?" My stomach fluttered.

"It's you. I don't know. There's something about you."

I broke eye contact and hopped out of bed in self-preservation.

"Apparently it's called Blank Canvas."

I crawled out of bed less confident than I'd thrown us into it, and we dressed in silence. On our way out I caught another glimpse of Dorothy and the gang. Off to see the wizard.

*****

"You're kidding me." I guffawed and slapped my knee for effect. "This has got to be a joke."

Enyo sat across from me, her legs crossed, unresponsive to my reaction… almost. Exasperation flashed across her face as she said, "Sam, I know this is overwhelming."

"Overwhelming? This is insane. You want me to kill the queen?"

"It's the only way," she said.

"Tough titties. I feel bad stepping on ants. I'm no assassin."

By uncrossing her legs to lean forward, Enyo eliminated the short distance between our two white stools. Brun-Brun had gone to a lot of trouble to get me here—another apparent honor to meet a bigwig in this world. This conversation must have been beneath her, and dealing with my un-pious reluctance surely made things worse.

"That disgusting thing you call the Queen of Witches plans to attack your world with an army of Spectrum-awakened soldiers."

"Look. I just got here! Some guy brought me trying to suck out my soul—." I looked down at my crotch.

"Sam, that's the whole point. The only thing you ever knew—your world—is powerless against an army trained here.

You've seen what the Spectrum can do. It won't be fair. It will be a slaughter."

I leaned back, recreating the distance Enyo had removed. "I don't even know if I believe you. The wand-waving glitter queen *I met* doesn't seem the fighting type."

"You're wrong."

"Well then, best of luck. You must really hate her—and sounds like you've got good reason—but since you're hiding in her Ivory Tower, why don't you walk up and deal with it yourself?"

For the first time, Enyo cracked a smile. I wished I'd stayed in my room, in bed… with Brun-Brun.

"The queen is my brother. I don't hate him, he's… misguided."

"Huh." I wondered how that might change things. "We've all got family issues, and I'm pretty sure your brother's your sister now anyway."

"Let's go back." Enyo crossed her legs again. "Maybe we jumped in too fast. Can you repeat back to me what I told you?" I dropped my chin, trying to communicate *are-you-serious*. "Humor me."

"The Queen of Witches, your sister," Enyo's lip flared, "is a diva ruling over a world I never knew existed, and she's raising an army of queers to destroy the world I do know exists."

"Yes." She nodded. "And what do you think?"

"I suppose that makes me uneasy."

"Why?"

"It's a little hard to place. Sure, war sounds bad, but this whole place makes me uneasy. Like, I can't shake the feeling that this chair might be filled with pixy dust waiting to levitate our teatime to the ceiling."

Enyo lightened up. "Took me a few years to get used to it. Back then it was different. No Ivory Tower. No city at all, just a bunch of gays hiding from reality."

"And the queen?"

"So he calls himself." That seemed to agitate her. "What did they tell you about unlocking your ability?"

I held up my Spectrum Guide. "Not much. Handed me this book and told me I'm basically on my own to practice and develop whatever I wanted."

She nodded, already aware. "The Spectrum isn't a test. It's the ultimate observation. The results are meant to guide you toward things that come naturally."

"But what does *Blank Canvas* mean?"

Enyo took my Spectrum Guide, and as she leafed through its empty pages, her face told me this was the first thing to happen she hadn't already expected.

"It means whatever you want it to mean. It means you can move things that get in your way, change minds that challenge you, build a tower that stretches farther than the eye can see, create a throne... or an army."

"The queen. She's a Blank Canvas?"

"Yes," she said and handed my Spectrum Guide back.

"What about you? Can you—."

Her headshake answered me before I finished. "It doesn't work like that."

Enyo paused to look me up and down.

"What?" I asked.

"I'm sad for you," she said.

"Why?"

"I was hoping you'd want to be a part of this."

"Sorry to disappoint. I want to help. I want to do the right thing, but I'm not going to kill someone. I don't have it in me."

"I understand. That's why I'm sad, because you don't have any choice."

I stood up. I didn't know anything about Enyo , and this conversation made me aware of her mystery and my vulnerability.

"I'm a Blank Canvas," I said. "I have all the choices, remember?"

"My brother did too, and he chose hate. You're in danger."

I turned to leave, and Enyo shouted after me, the alarm in her voice scaring the shit out of me. "Hatred festers. Love cleans. My brother will come for you. He'll find your hate, and use it to manipulate you."

"I don't hate my home," I said to myself, resisting the urge to look back.

Brun-Brun waited, along with two guards, on the other side of the exit. Thrusting the door open, Enyo's shouting poured over them.

"He'll come for you!" she shrieked, and I slammed the door shut.

The guards looked confused, and Brun-Brun ran to me.

"What happened?" he asked. "What was all that shouting?"

My pulse was rushing. I had never been so thankful for a door. She'd done what she wanted. She'd gotten inside my head. *You don't have any choice.*

"I need to get out of here. Take me back to the Transpo Hub. I took the Spectrum. I can use the doors, right?" I took Brun-Brun's hand, cognizant of the guards, and led him toward the backside of the faux mirror we'd passed through to reach Enyo's hideout. "It's not safe for me to be here."

"This is a safe place," he said. "Nobody knows about it."

"I don't mean this room. I mean this world!"

"Sam, I want to help. Tell me what happened. What did she say?"

Brun-Brun looked scared, but ready to help, *wanting* to help.

"She asked me to kill the queen."

"I thought she might," he said.

"She also said I didn't have a choice, that the queen would come for me. Then she chased me out, shouting about love."

"I don't get it," Brun-Brun said.

"You're telling me! She's nuts! Kept calling the queen her brother. I don't want to get in the middle of their family feud. I don't want anything to do with this!"

"We'll get you back," he said.

"Really?"

"I don't know what happened in that room, but I heard her shouting." He smiled. "Plus, you look terrible."

I let out a half-laugh, releasing a little of the pounding stress that compressed my insides.

"Brun-Brun, you wanted me to meet with her. What will happen? With her army? The war? Everything you told me?"

Brun-Brun kissed me, and the butterflies returned. This was real. It was fast, and wreckless, and poorly timed, but I kissed him back.

"We'll figure it out," he said. "Come on. The Transpo Hub isn't far."

Chapter 18

Echoing Cavern

I sprinted out of the control room before the queen cut her transmission. Renegayd had become more extreme, but the queen's meeting with the Global Rights Organization chucked the frog straight into the flames. I had to get out.

"Adele, you can't come with me!"

"You think I want to be part of this?" she said, sprinting passed me to press the elevator down button.

"But the Scales—" I said.

"Are you kidding? The queen blew people's dicks off—on camera—as a warning." *Ding.* The elevator arrived. "So what the fuck do we do?"

"We have to find her sister," I said jabbing the button for my floor. "Enyo's our best shot. Get whatever you need and meet me in front of the Ivory Tower. We'll find someplace to hide and figure out how to find her."

The times I'd seen Enyo were irreproducible: when I'd chanced into her at the Transpo Hub, when she'd appeared in my room, and when Brun-Brun took me to her. We were searching for someone who didn't want to be found, not by a member of the Scales of Justice.

Adele got out at her floor, and the elevator descended a few more. I half expected to see the queen waiting for me in the hallway; instead, the doors opened to the empty, fluorescent-lit B-corridor leading to room 314. My Spectrum Guide only confirmed that my canvas remained blank, but I threw it into a knapsack anyway. War with the queen would mean I needed to become useful. My room had served as an escape from insanity for nearly a year. Both worlds had changed since I first arrived. This world, which had welcomed with awe, had become allergic to me, threatening to destroy everything.

A soft *pfft* sound accompanied a burst of dazzling color.

"Goin' somewhere?"

Smiling next to the *Wizard of Oz* poster, the queen blocked the exit.

"I don't want anything to do with this anymore."

"But we're just getting started!" she cheered.

"You're just getting started. You and the Scales have still got everything. *Please* let me go."

"Why?"

"Um, because you threatened the world with testicle fingers, and because I get the feeling you'd rather kill me than let me go."

She didn't seem to connect the absurdity of where she'd been minutes ago, of what she'd done to Mission Morality, and how deranged Renegayd looked to the rest of the world.

"I can take you to Brun-Brun." The way she said it sucked out all potential joy. "Right in the middle of the rainbow."

I didn't believe her. "Let me go!"

"You don't want to see him? You been searching for that boy for months. I offer to take you straight to him, and that's your response? What happened to us?" She laughed.

"You said you didn't know where he was."

"I lied," she said.

"Yeah, a lot."

"Not a lot! Just the unsavory bits. Things you needn't worry your pretty little head about."

"Ha! Well, *that's* what happened to us."

"What are you going to do if I let you go? Find my sister? Join forces and take down Renegayd?"

"I don't think we'll have to. You're doing a fine job running it into the ground all on your own."

"You have so little faith in your own world."

"Our world," I corrected. "And I have no clue what you're talking about."

"*With us or against us.* Isn't that what the Scales of Justice was proving the whole time? That every day of inequality causes harm. You know better than anyone that there are two sides to this equation."

There was no point in arguing. The Scales had argued it all.

"Please, let me go," I tried.

"SAM?" A voice startled the queen from the other side of my door.

"Adele!" I screamed. "Help! The queen—"

A surge of heat blasted the door off the hinges and slammed the queen against the wall.

"Sam, come on!" Adele shouted.

I didn't see Dionysia beneath the rubble of Adele's surprise attack, but I wasn't going to look. Slinging my knapsack over my shoulder, I took one hard step on the ruined doorway and grabbed Adele's hand. We ran for the elevator.

"I think I know where Brun-Brun is," I said. "He can help us find Enyo."

"Where?"

"You have to trust me."

Ding.

In the lobby, the waterfall's mist refracted a full rainbow across the gaudy room.

"Hey!" Benj, and the rest of the Scales of Justice called to us from across the room.

There wasn't time to talk.

"Trust me," I said and grabbed Adele's hand.

"What are we doing?!" Adele screamed, but she ran with me, straight for the pool of water beneath the waterfall.

"What are you doing?!" The Scales shouted from across the room.

Adele and I reached the end of the path and jumped straight for the falling water, beneath the very middle of the rainbow. Mist tickled my face as we hurtled through falling water, but instead of plunging into the pool beneath the falls, my feet tripped on solid ground. We face-planted on solid ground.

"Oof! What the hell?" Adele jumped up, hands ignited for defense. "Where are we?"

Adele's voice echoed down an unfinished rock tunnel descending into darkness. Behind us, the lobby had disappeared, the waterfall entrance replaced by a rock wall. There was no sound or smell of rushing water. The wall blocked everything.

"Solid," I confirmed, testing the wall by pressing against it.

"Awwwooooo!" A furry creature flew through the wall my hand rested against and knocked me down the tunnel's gradual slope.

"Benj?" Adele ran to him as he shape-shifted back into our beefy friend.

"What about the rest?" I asked.

He ran back to the rock wall and tested its solidness for himself.

"They're with the queen," he said with a slight quiver. "I tried convincin' 'em, but—."

A third body materialized from the wall, falling straight into Benj's arms.

"Shǎng!"

Benj wrapped Shǎng in his hulking embrace. Anxious, but hopeful, we waited until it was obvious no one else was coming. No Lou. No Jacob.

"Boy, you better have a plan!" Shǎng said, holding Benj's hand.

"Rescue Brun-Brun and join Enyo." I said, trying to sound sure of myself.

"Oh Jesus." Shǎng joked. "This better be one hell of a man. Adele, can we get some light?"

Adele laughed.

"It's not just about him!" I tried.

"Whatever."

Maybe it wasn't a coincidence that the Scales of Justice

fractured between old and new members, leaving the original four—a Werewolf, a Flamer, an Empath, and me—to trudge the Ivory Tower's dark, dank, completely unfabulous underbelly.

*****

My feeling of being pursued by the queen waned the further we went. I told everyone everything, admitting I didn't know what we were looking for, but that I was sure Brun-Brun was here somewhere. Brun-Brun could take us to the queen's sister, and from there we could work against Renegayd.

"Too late to turn back anyway," Benj said. "Queen'll sniff out anyone against what she's doin'. It was either join you or have her realize we're still sane."

"Debatable," Shǎng said.

Benj pulled him closer and squeezed his shoulder.

"Ow!"

They laughed, and the resulting echo changed farther down the tunnel.

"Adele. Send the light down there."

Our dragonfly torch drifted ahead, leaving darkness to creep around us.

"Whoa…" Shǎng said. "I'm feeling a lot."

"A lot of what?" Adele shfited her hand controlling our light source.

"There's— there's people here, somewhere. A lot of them."

The walls of the tunnel disappeared, and a cavern devoured our dragonfly, its light unable to touch anything but darkness. The path dead-ended at a cliff, which the four of us crowded to see below.

"Adele," I said. "We need more light."

She ignited her hands, and generated an intensifying glow by rubbing her hands together.

"Get back!"

Pushing the heat from her body, she channeled fire through her outstretched arms into the black abyss. A pillar of fire unveiled the surrounding area. There was a pit at the bottom, filled with metallic objects that danced in the thrashing flames high above.

"There's people down there!" Shǎng said, using his Empath ability to fill us in. "But… they're prisoners!"

I squinted, trying to make out the metal objects: iron cages, attached to the ceiling by long chains that stirred as people charged the bars of their cells to look up at us.

"Brun-Brun!" I shouted. "Brun-Brun! Are you here?"

Murmurs echoed up from the pit, turning into shouts as hundreds of prisoners awoke.

One voice rose above the rest. "SAM!?"

"Brun-Brun! It's me!"

"I can't keep this up!" Adele shouted.

The fire extinguished at her arms first before curling up the pillar like a fuse that returned the cavern to darkness. Almost darkness. A new glow remained in front of the cliff, floating in the middle of the cavern… self-contained, with something at its center.

"Shit!" cried Shǎng. "It's her!"

The queen floated above the prison floor, illuminated by her canary, sheath dress.

"Hooray!" The queen's wand ejaculated a few pathetic streamers as she twirled it. "You found each other. I just *love* reunions."

The prisoners cursed and screamed beneath her while the queen surveyed the pit.

"SHUT UP!" she replied, amplifying her voice to near-eardrum-bursting level until it was quiet. "I *told* you I'd take you to him. Then Fire-Crotch clobbered me with a door, *ruining* our chance to chat. No matter. Here we are. The Scales of Justice and the truth behind their pristine revolution."

"We've worked together for years! How can you do this?" Benj shouted from the cliff's edge.

"We did this together! All of us. These are the outliers to your equations. Forgotten. None of you thought that maybe a few teensy-weensy problems might pop up in our own world."

"These people. They're all Renegayd?" Adele asked.

"Renegayd hasn't been around forever… but in spirit, yes, they were. Then, they stopped cooperating. Unimportant variables clouding moral certainty."

"You've been imprisoning people? This whole time!" I was horrified by the size of the room.

"And you liked it that way!" the queen hissed. "As you should, just the people seeking reassurance with the ones who provide it. Up in your tower, debating the heart of the issue: right versus wrong."

"*This* is wrong!" I shouted.

"Oh, please! This doesn't change anything. Your equations were overwhelmingly clear. A few people wouldn't change the outcome. It was easier to tidy house so you could focus on your work."

Like everything, we could turn the issue around and around.

"I don't care!" I said. "It doesn't matter how much you've thought through this!"

The queen floated above it all. "Blank Canvas no longer cares about morality?"

"That's right," I said.

She chewed on the thought. "The low road, mmm? Doing whatever you want—right or wrong. A wildcard."

She was quiet, and then her wand jolted back by her side as she jumped back to life.

"I like it! I think that's a grand idea. And you'll start with an army! You'd like that, eh?" She shouted down into the pit, "You want out of here?" Threats and name-calling from the horde beneath sounded like affirmation from up here. "Then it's settled."

She placed the tip of her wand against her lips and blew; it emitted a cheap birthday "ha*zuhh*" noise as its opposite end unrolled. As the trick raveled back into the wand, a horrible grinding replaced it. The queen turned her attention to the pit.

"Sam DeSalvo has convinced me to release you. Sam DeSalvo is your savior! Got that? You owe your freedom to him."

Cheering erupted in the darkness, and their faceless joy nourished a tiny feeling of hope. "Sam!" they shouted, spilling out of their cages. It became rhythmic, echoing. "Sam. Sam. Sam."

"Broccoli Top," the queen said, somehow above the crowd and maybe only to me. "Life's more interesting with you in it."

She winked, twirled, did a little dance, and disappeared in her signature spew of glitter. The grinding continued, and my dread grew as each iron cage lifted, turning freed prisoners into what the queen had promised: an army.

Someone patted me on the back.

"Guess, you did it. Brun-Brun is free!"

The Ivory Tower

Chapter 5

Love's Detour

"I feel bad," Brun-Brun said, squeezing my shoulder as we exited the Ivory Tower. "I shouldn't have taken you to Enyo."

"No, I'm shitty. I'm sure there's a better way to handle this, but it's my first time in a magic world with a hot prince helping me escape an evil queen."

"Hot prince, eh?"

"And funny. And strong." I took a minute to check him out. "Sexy as hell. Jesus! What's wrong with me? Shouldn't I be running toward all this? Saving the world?"

"Yeah, I see what you mean. You are a shitty person." Brun-Brun led us back past Pansy's Pub-erty. "You're doing the best you can."

"Come back with me," I urged.

His smile wilted. "Someone has to try and stop her."

"You really believe she's building an army?" I asked. "Yes,

clearly you do. God, you must think I'm the worst. I'm literally refusing to help, and you're willing to—what—die for this? It's not even your world!"

"My world's attacking. Feels like I've got to at least try to make things better. The queen's pushing your world into this. Being a bystander here feels wrong."

"That makes so much sense!" I stopped and looked behind us, up at the enormous Ivory Tower, which disappeared into the haze of perception. "If what you're saying is true—."

"Sam, stop. You haven't had a lifetime here. Enyo told you the queen's plan, but you don't *know* any of it. All you know is what you see and what you've been told."

"What about what I *feel*?"

"What *do* you feel?" Brun-Brun asked.

"I feel like you're a good person, but what do I do if I believe you? Try to learn a magic power and kill the queen?"

"I know you'll do the right thing," he said.

"Sounds like you want me to stay."

"I want you to be safe."

"And you don't think going back to my world is safe, right? Because she's going to attack it soon anyway?"

"That's what you're saying," Brun-Brun answered. "I said I want you to be safe. I wanted you to meet Enyo, because I thought she could help keep you safe. If that's not the right plan, then you have to make your own."

"She told me her sister was going to come for me. She told me to kill the queen!"

"So... we're running away! What do you want from me? Sam, don't tell me I'm a prince and then turn your back. It's not fair."

With the statue of the closet door coming into view, a commotion rose at the front of Transpo Hub Square. Brun-Brun grabbed my hand and yanked me into a nearby shop.

"Everything alright, boys?" the grey-haired owner welcomed us from behind the counter.

"Fine," Brun-Brun said without looking away from the window.

Outside the concrete arches of the hub's open-air chamber were hundreds of people, all wearing rainbow vests.

"What's going on? Who are all those people?"

"We're too late," he said. "She's started."

"That's her army?"

They didn't seem threatening. I examined the closest member of the rainbow brigade: male, about my age, spiked-up black hair, jeans, and a rainbow vest, no undershirt. Nothing menacing or out of the ordinary, except for a small holster on his waist.

"He's armed. See that thing on his belt?" I said.

"Hooligans!" The shop owner appeared behind us. "Been there for hours."

The group stirred, their attention turning to the closet-filled Transpo Hub, until our view of the rectangular portals leading to every gayborhood in my world was replaced by the backs of rainbow vests.

"What are they doing?" I asked. "Are they going to attack?"

"Attack what?" said the shop owner.

"I think so," Brun-Brun answered. "They're reaching for the holster,"

They raised their weapons above their heads. "They look… happy?"

"Damned if they don't look excited!" said the shop owner.

They started jumping, and as their roar grew, the crowd parted to create a path leading out of the hub.

"Somethin's comin' out!"

Multicolored petals bloomed above the crowd as a bouquet of rose, fuchsia, and buttercup mists exploded from their hands. A new group of people in rainbow vests ran out of Transpo Hub, high-fiving the line, as the colored clouds descended.

"What in tarnation?" said the shop owner, and the tiny bell jingled as he ran out to investigate.

"Brun-Brun?" I asked.

He looked confused. The group was hugging and cheering. They weren't holding weapons, but cans of spray paint. This wasn't an army. It was a sports team celebrating a victory. The cloud of paint drifted our direction, covering the shop owner as he spun with arms overhead, transforming into a speckled ornament.

The crowd boomed as the queen appeared, beaming in a tight, black dress marked by two long streaks of paint. Her army was jubilant but delicate with their queen, leaving a cushion of space around her as she passed under the Transpo Hub arch laughing, pointing, and nodding, a celebrity on her rainbow carpet.

"Sam, we should get out of here," Brun-Brun said. "Sam?"

Though the cheers grew louder, my mind dulled its thunder. With each step the queen took through the gauntlet it became clear she was headed straight toward the shop.

She was staring at us, extending her hand, she wagged one long fingernail, beckoning us to come outside. The jingling bell made some part of my mind realize I was leaving the shop, but I was unable to stop. Brun-Brun whispered under his breath at my side, but I didn't—or couldn't—process what he said.

"My Gumdrops!" she cried. "There you two are!"

Something broke the trance, launching me back into the reality of standing across from the woman I'd been asked to kill. The woman I was told would be coming for me.

I stumbled and looked at Brun-Brun.

"My Queen." He bowed.

"Oh, stop that, B! What about this moment seems appropriate for bowing?" She wrapped her speckled black arms around me, smearing paint on my shirt. "Oh! Sorry, Sugar! It's still fresh! I never told you congratulations on completing your Spectrum test. Welcome to the family. This is how coming out should feel, like one hell of a party!"

"Ha. Yeah, thanks." I tried to act normal. Lucky for me, *overwhelmed* was my natural expression.

"I wanted to chat." She was nonchalant.

"Sure. I mean, clearly this isn't the right time."

"Honey Bear, bein' queen means it's always the right time." I silently begged Brun-Brun for help. "You lovebirds! Brun-Brun, we'll meet you at the tower. Come along, Sam."

With a lazy twirl, her wand spit a burst of glitter in my face.

"Pfoot! Gyaa!"

I brushed away glitter and saw that the crowd—along with the street, the shop owner, Brun-Brun, and the whole commotion—had vanished. We weren't in Transpo Hub Square anymore. Instead, the queen was perched above me, her rainbow paint now regal in the lights of her throne room.

"Hey there, Mint Gum. Heard you got your results from that hunk of a man, Benj. Woof. Ha! Get it?"

"Where's Brun-Brun?" I asked. "How did we get here?"

The queen ignored my questions, but not the subject. "You two sure hooked up quick. That Brun-Brun… always after the Castro portal boys." Her words stirred jealousy I didn't expect. "I mean, who can blame you for wanting to try the local flavor? Gorgeous, smooth talker… like a conman. Look, I'm no bullshitter. I know you've seen my sister. Tried to find you when I heard about the whole Blank Canvas thing. Assumed Enyo was involved when I couldn't. By the look on your face, I think I'm right." She fiddled with something in her lap while she spoke. "Wish you'd tell me where she was so I could sort things out between us, but she prefers sending her minions."

"I don't know what you're talking about," I tried.

"Sure." She popped a piece of gum in her mouth. "So, what'd she tell you? I'll guess… How 'bout Attack Plans for a hundred dollars? Ding ding ding! Attacking your world—my world too."

"I *don't* know what you're talking about," I repeated.

Dionysia, the Queen of Witches, stomped her stiletto, sending an echo through the throne room as she stood. I felt small beneath her throne, in her tower, in her world. There was nothing in my reach except two tall, metal candleholders flanking the five steps separating her throne from the floor where I stood. The queen took a step down. I jumped for the left candleholder and swung the long rod, unsure if I hoped to ignite her with the candle or joust with the whole thing.

"Well, damn! Like that, eh? Gonna lay a smack down?"

"Don't— don't come any closer. What's going on? What

happened at the Transpo Hub? Is that your army?"

She seemed amused. "I heard people're calling it that. I like the ring of it. I mean, what queen doesn't want an army? And you're a Blank Canvas… figures. I knew there was a whole lot goin' on in there."

She pointed her wand up and down and took another step. My body tensed with the weight of the candleholder.

"Why are you doing this?" I asked. "Why are you attacking your own world?"

"What kind of animal destroys her own home?"

"Enyo said you ran to this world, made yourself queen, and started training an army for revenge."

Something about what I'd said made the queen seethe. She took another step—only two more before we were on equal ground.

"This's got nothin' to do with revenge. Your Spectrum results pin you as awfully gullible. You don't see convention, so you jump on whatever bandwagon comes to town."

"I don't care what your test says. I make my own choices."

"Please. Everybody thinks they're special until they read their results and realize the Spectrum's got 'em pegged. Unique, but not unknowable. I read your results."

"You don't know everything!" I said, and jammed the candleholder forward.

The queen dodged my pitiful jab, poking the air with her wand. The candleholder slipped from my grasp and glued itself to the steps without bouncing, as if magnetized to the ground.

"I know enough to know you ain't gonna kill me. Not in your D-N-A." She smacked her gum. "These people born here don't understand what it's like for you and me."

The queen changed as she advanced out of the spotlight and onto the ground level. For the first time, she looked normal; she looked tired.

"Your sister warned me you'd come once you heard about my results."

"She said that, huh? Seems wonderfully clear to have it laid out so black and white. Enyo's good, The Queen of Witches is evil."

"I think she called you *misguided*."

"Ha! The nerve." The queen shook off her reaction. "Imagine what it would be like if you'd been born here, to a world where being queer is normal. Where nobody looks at you different because of who you are. Don't you think it would have been better?"

It was hard not to agree. People here didn't spend time thinking about their sexuality. It was everywhere and nowhere. There was no need to hide it or to reveal it. Here, everyone just lived, because they could.

"This world isn't perfect," I said. "I don't feel discriminated against back home, either."

"You don't notice chains standing still. I'm not even talking about perfect. I'm talking about decent."

"You can't convince me that attacking our world is the *right* thing to do. What made you hate it so much?"

"I've had pain, but I've been through that fire and emerged a diamond. This isn't retaliation; it's liberation. This isn't about my hate. It's about everyone else's."

"Everyone? Seems like plenty of progress is being made. The

Supreme Court ruled in favor of gay marriage!" I protested.

"Sure! A reward for desiring heteronormatives. Special laws, state-sanctioned discrimination. Justice Kennedy sait it: 'Outlaw to outcast may be a step forward, but it does not achieve the full promise of liberty.' It's blinding you! Imprisoning all of us! Grindr profiles all read the same: *Masc. Straight acting. No femmes or fatties. HIV-neg, UB2. Be discreet.* What progress! That double take on the street, a discounted meal because someone wants you to know they don't mind your gayness... that's discrimination! I want to pay the same as everyone else."

"That's ridiculous."

"You're right. I'll take the free lunch, but I don't have to like it."

"It's a step," I said.

"Is it? 1966. Your city! The cops tried pushin' a drag queen out of Compton's Cafeteria. God love her, that queen threw her coffee at them in protest, and the whole place joined in. Lipstick flyin', bags beat upside their heads. Havoc in the Tenderloin."

"And now drag queens drink coffee in peace!" I replied.

"Aren't we lucky for a pinhole view of the world! They don't in South Carolina, Missy! Or Texas, or Mississippi, or even some places in your so-called progressive city. Shit's still broke there too. You never been wronged in San Francisco?"

I had. Several times. But I wouldn't give her the satisfaction of agreeing.

"Things gotta change!" she continued. "You wait. 'Traditional values' is the next victim. Bigots feeling discriminated against by labels of bigotry. They're just sayin' what they think, after all. Ain't nothin' wrong with that. Except of course, it is wrong! Kids hear that shit and kill themselves rather than tell Mommy and Daddy.

Look at the world. How many countries have even a fraction of what you're content with?"

"Whatever," I said.

"Oh good! Your limits of care for life and liberty met in five minutes!"

"It's like arguing with a crazy person!" I said, unable to pinpoint the madness outside my disgust for the whole conversation. "You've made your mind up."

"You accept the harm done to *our* side, but get your britches in a bunch by the idea of balancing the scales?"

"By killing people?" I asked, testing Brun-Brun's warning.

"I'm for violence if nonviolence means postponing a solution—just to avoid violence. I'm a reasonable woman. Tell me a better way."

This was not a physical or mental battle I was capable of winning. I didn't know anything about liberation. In that way she was right: I had a pinhole view of the world, and I liked it.

The queen saved me from my own silence. "There hasn't been a single successful civil rights movement without a militant arm. It's not a new idea. Stonewall sparked the foundation of the Gay Liberation Front, which fought—using whatever necessary—for change. Then, we got tunnel vision—forgot how bad things still are, forgot we didn't want assimilation, but liberty. Renegayd is Sylvia Rivera's beer bottle. We're restarting the rebellion. Gay rights is a familiar story playing over again. We all know we're headed for equality. Problem is we're taking for-*fucking*-ever to get there."

"We've been *faster* than other movements. We learned from them!"

"Faster? People been gay since we crawled out the ocean on our bellies. We're the dog of civil rights: happy with a few crumbs of humanity as conciliation for rolling over. Your back's to your family because you live in California. People are dying. Children are dying! Every second we stand by, waiting for change, they're being killed or killing themselves. You know we only see the half of it."

"Nobody thinks that's okay," I said.

"But no one is doing anything about it!"

"Tons of people work for equality every day."

"Well." She pointed her wand straight at me. "I say it's time we demand it. Whatever it takes. Equality means balancing the equation—we make things equal. Our side's been in the red too long. Faster change means less pain. Think of the harm we can avoid for every day we speed up equality. Let's say the world reaches equality in five hundred years. Perfect equality. Like here, where no one thinks about gender or sexuality. So much good will come from speeding that up: victims with no bullies, prisoners with no persecutors, *deaths* with no reason. The sadness and pain that comes with it… all avoided."

Her conviction, the path she described… it was frightening to see an unstable mind and understand it.

"But you would kill people on the other side of the equation? You feel justified?"

"Not if we don't have to. But can't you feel the urgency? We're racing to save people in torment. Radical good permits radicalism. Just balancing an equation. If we can do that with only addition, we'll do it."

"Who are you going to fight?" I asked. "Everyone?"

"Why? You wanna help me strategize?" She smiled.

"I want to stop you!"

"Oh! Is that why you're running for the Transpo Hub? Off to stop me from the comfort of your pinhole?" She was right, but hearing it confused everything. "It ain't easy, Prickly Pear. Put your big boy pants on. If our fight for human dignity *is* the same story, then there's plenty of examples to follow. American civil rights had Black Panthers, Soul Students Advisory Council, and the Revolutionary Action Movement. Feminism's sure sprinkled with radicals. Hell even the tree huggers got Deep Green Resistance. Pick your *saveur de résistance*."

"Haven't we seen those fail?" My limited knowledge came pouring out. "I'm pretty sure we *know* nonviolence is the way. Civil disobedience, MLK Jr, Gandhi, Nelson Mandela!"

"Sure, peace gets the victory, but it's too damn slow. The verbal abuse, the beating, the homelessness, suicide, incarceration… it needs to stop. The LGBT movement *needs* us."

A tear picked up flecks of glitter as it fell down her cheek.

"You can't destroy the world to make it equal."

"You got it ass-backward, don't you? What you saw at Transpo Hub Square, that was our coming out. That look like murderers to you? Spray paint, limp-wristed high-fives, and grab-ass? We ain't destroying anything but hate. We're makin' a statement; one only our fabulous group of gays can make."

I'd wanted a drink at a bar, maybe a rebound, but this… this was something big. Or it could be. Her army wasn't full of soldiers; it was full of activists. She didn't mean to destroy the world; she meant to change it… for the better.

I tried to argue. "I don't think this is the way—"

"But you don't know for sure that it isn't. Look, you're on the right side of two worlds. *This* one's about doin' whatever you want. What kind of revolutionist would I be if everyone on my team was there against their will?"

The queen had caught me off guard. I was ready for lies—for insanity—but not for heartbroken logic. I felt myself disappointing some inner fantasy of how things *should* be as my mind found pieces of what she said to be true. I didn't know what to say. This was wrong, but I didn't know if it was *more* wrong than letting things keep going the way they were going. Slow progress had a cost. Faster change was good.

"It could make things worse." My voice quivered, embarrassed by its own feeble objection.

"Reactions to what we do will show how far we need to go. My sister lied to you, Buttercup. She and whoever else you been listenin' to are tellin' you I'm gonna destroy everything, because they need you. I've been straight—err—honest with you. Renegayd's on a tough road, but our cause is pure. Perfect Equality, like here."

She smiled, and a dull roar seeped into the throne room. She looked toward the exit, the back of her fairy door. Standing on the blood-red tile walkway beneath her throne, I was all that stood between her and that exit.

"You don't have to come, but you still wanna kill me?"

I stepped to the side, defeated. "I…."

"Oh, you were fabulous! Points for effort… and for *style*! Very sexy. Provin' you got brains to go with that big dose of manly brawn."

Her heels clicked as she passed me. Then the sound stopped,

and I turned around to see her bedazzled hand outstretched.

"So, you coming?" she asked.

I touched my fingertips to hers, and hand in hand we walked out of the throne room to meet the queen's army returning from battle.

"Watch the fingernails, Sugar."

Chapter 6

Orgiastic Flute Melodies

We hugged when Brun-Brun found me in the crowded Ivory Tower lobby.

"I was worried she'd gotten you," he said.

My conversation with the queen had made me mad—embarrassed! How could I be manipulated so easily? Falling for someone—believing the crap he and Enyo fed me. The queen didn't feel dangerous. She felt determined. She felt sad. I didn't know if I liked what she was doing, but at least she was honest.

"She didn't *get* me. We just talked. It was… enlightening."

"What does that mean? Where are we going?" Brun-Brun followed me, shouting over the pounding techno beat of the celebration that had paraded in from the Transpo Hub.

"We're checking it out," I said at normal volume, not caring if he could hear me.

Orgie flowed freely. The lobby waterfall had transformed,

spraying a mist of it into the air, the rainbow the only thing unchanged about it. People lined both sides of the river, filling cups or jumping in. The group's bottled tension had fermented and blown its top into pure debauchery.

The celebration in the Ivory Tower was chaotic, but when we emerged onto Main Street the party's true scale was overwhelming. The tower itself was alive, lit up like Disney's Electric Parade. Vapor oozed from the main doors, and lasers danced in the sky. Everyone was marked by spray paint. One man's arms and legs had been painted one color each. Another danced in a white wedding dress turned canvas for the surrounding crowd.

A slurring, shirtless boy stumbled into me. He sprayed a blotch of bright orange paint on my chest, handed me an electric-lime drink, and then clinked our plastic cups.

"T' Renegayd!" he managed before disappearing back into the mob.

I looked at Brun-Brun. His forehead scrunched.

"What are you doing?" he asked. "I thought you wanted to go home."

A swig of Orgie brought tingling to the ends of each limb.

"The queen doesn't want to destroy the world," I shouted. "She wants to change it for the better! It's a political movement, not an army!"

Brun-Brun attempted a half-whisper over the music. "It's not safe here."

"You're wrong."

Brun-Brun grabbed my arm. "What's gotten into you? What happened with you and the queen?"

I wanted to ask, *Why didn't you tell me she wanted to create equality?* Or even, *Why didn't you tell me the truth—the whole story?* But another question slipped out instead. "What happened with you and the last guy to come through the Castro portal?"

"What?"

"I hear you welcome everyone who comes through. I'm curious. Do you tell them *all* this shit about their world being in danger? Weird fetish, but points for creativity."

He was angry, and I liked seeing it. I wanted to prove I could manipulate him too.

"*You* threw *me* on the bed, remember?" he said.

"Oh please. Isn't that how it always goes?"

"Why are you doing this?" he asked.

"Doing the best I can," I mocked. "To Renegayd!"

He grabbed my arm and tried to sell me one last time. "Sam, the queen's using you! She's trying to get close, because she knows you're a threat. A Blank Canvas. You can stop her."

I took another sip, and had my delight, before replying. "I don't want to stop her. I'm going to help her. You're the one trying to use me."

He looked at me like a stranger, or like the strangers we were. "Nobody knew you were a Blank Canvas until your test!" he shouted. "You know what's at stake, and all you can think about is the last guy I fucked?"

He smacked the bottom of my cup, spraying Orgie everywhere as it somersaulted through the air, and then stomped off. I hadn't noticed the scene we'd caused until staring faces surrounded me. The circle collapsed, hugging and consoling me, wiping Orgie off my forehead.

"You go, honey!"

"What a jerk!"

"Asshole!" someone shouted after him.

"Here." Another cup appeared before me. "To new beginnings."

Clink. And the swell rushed over.

Someone in the outer limits grabbed my ass. I followed the hand, still glued to my left cheek, and found it connected to a dark, handsome, scruffy man who winked before dipping a slender glass tube into his cup, raising it above his head, and dripping a few drops of Orgie straight into his eye. His hand released my ass as he convulsed in ecstasy. His smile stretched larger than life as he shouted in my ear, "Straight to the brain, Chico!"

He held the dropper over me, and I leaned back. C'est la vie.

Drinking Orgie was a splash of instant orgasm. Dripping it was a geyser, shooting pleasure in places I'd never felt. The force faded, but unlike drinking, the electricity lingered.

The crowd had turned. There were dancers on every climbable surface. A persistent electronic beat pumped life into the amorphous disco, and it consumed me. Sweat and dancing. Hands and groping. Lights and Orgie. The mass parted to reveal a grey-haired man on his knees, jaw unhinged, before that window closed and another opened to reveal two women squashing a third between their spray-painted breasts.

Some had sex. Some watched. Others did drugs. It wasn't hard to recognize. Popping pills and tabs; snorting dust and fumes, injecting liquids…. The orifices were familiar, but this party put it together like I'd never seen.

It was Folsom Street Fair times the infinite floors of the Ivory Tower.

"Sam. Sam! Over here!" The dancing mob somehow ejaculated my hulking Spectrum proctor, who waved me over with one massive, werewolf hand. His other arm was occupied by an Asian boy dangling from his bicep. "Congratulations!"

He extended his cup, and we cheers'd. A third cup crashed into ours.

"Hiii. I'm Shǎnguāng."

Benj lowered his arm to set the dangling boy down.

"Great to meet you," I said.

"Great to meet yoouu," he replied, drunk.

Benj nuzzled Shǎnguāng before reattaching their mouths. A woman with color-streaked hair grabbed my neck to yell in my ear.

"Adele!" She put out her fist.

"Sam!" And we fist-bumped. Adele's long hair fell over her shoulders and covered half her rainbow vest.

"Sam jus inish is Spectrum tes!" Benj murmured from the side of his mouth not kissing Shǎnguāng.

"Thanks for the introduction," Adele said rolling her eyes and turning to me. "Congrats. So, what do you think?"

"I don't know," I admitted. "Pretty wild!"

The conversation felt out of body, or I did. Intense pleasure vibrated over my thoughts, fighting for attention.

"Feels wrong!" she replied.

"What do you mean?"

"Appear out of thin air, spray paint the white house, and run back to another world? To party?"

"That's what happened?" I managed.

"Feels cheap!"

Half dancing to avoid standing like a statue on the street-become-dance-floor, Adele broke eye contact. Her gaze was over my shoulder, on a dark-haired figure in black stilettos strapped up to her knee like spiderwebs. The black widow woman stood in the middle of a circle, her blue dress marked by a diagonal, green stripe. Reeled in, Adele joined her audience with me following after.

"And then, ve busted gate and stormed the Kremlin. It vas quite ze scene of course. FSB does not like gays, but to see an army of us—and charging ze Kremlin... zey opened fire immediately." Her lips curled up, and she blinked twice, adding suspense. "Unfortunate for them Vlad reverses trajectory of moving objects."

Someone jostled the web, interrupting with, "You killed them?"

The Russian examined the interruption, contemplating a strike, and then tossed her hair. "If afraid of wolves, don't go to woods. This vas risk. Small cost for hope. Ze government rob me of my rights. Ve take them back."

Adele yanked me out of the circle and pried Benj and Shǎnguāng apart. She pointed at the Russian circle.

"Did you hear? Renegayd killed people at the Kremlin."

"It's too bad," Benj said.

"Too bad?" Adele yelled.

Maybe it was the Orgie, or my fight with Brun-Brun, or my conversation with Dionysia, but I tried on the queen's logic: "Was it worth it?"

"What do you mean?" Adele said.

"I mean, was the good we accomplished worth the bad? That

woman said so herself. The Russian government isn't exactly innocent in the LGBT arena."

Adele scrunched her nose. "I don't know Sam. Why don't you tell me?"

"Just saying, it might have been worth it."

Benj nodded. "Ends justify the means."

"I'm uncomfortable assuming that." Adele crossed her arms.

Benj seemed to appreciate that. Then someone bumped me, and I took a sip to avoid spilling. Looking back up, I saw someone cute. My shirt felt soft.

"Hey!" Adele shouted. "You okay?"

"Balance the equation," I blurted out, attempting to stay connected. "Make sure we didn't go too far."

Pleasure blocked all other senses. I looked into my cup, trying to center myself in the bright liquid. The vibration amplified across my body.

Benj grabbed my shoulder, anchoring me in reality. "...know what we're doin' is worth it."

I nodded violently, trying to mirror Benj and hide that I was losing control.

A six-pack beneath a ripped tank top finally tore my attention from the group. I gave up resisting. Stumbling forward, the crowd ate my eye candy and spat out another. This one noticed me too. He rubbed my arm. His hand was soft. Lips softer. I opened my eyes, and he was gone. Nothing was familiar; even my body beat with unfamiliar sensations. The music came to an abrupt halt, and I tried to stand still to match.

"Welcome, everyone!" the queen's voice boomed, returning some soundtrack to the lights' continued dancing. "Welcome

Renegayd! I'm so proud of all you dysfunctional weirdos." People cheered. "And misfits." More cheering. "And *QUEERS!*"

At that, the crowd erupted. I looked for the queen, but couldn't see beyond her subjects.

"Tonight marks the beginning of our liberation..." Even with her booming, amplified voice I had trouble concentrating. "This wonderful place we call home is fab-u-lous. But it ain't reality for most of us. Today proved that. Our... *victorious* coming out was not unchallenged. The Russian Kremlin, South Korea's Blue House, Casa Rosada in Argentina, the Dominican Republic's National Palace...... of the forty global capitols where we announced Renegayd...."

Was the crowd still dancing?

"...that—ladies, gentlemen, and in-betweens—that's what today was about.... Today, you gave one hell of a bitch slap to hate and one nasty-ass tongue-in-mouth to love. For God's sake, let's get to lovin' ourselves!"

In kicked the music, and up went the energy.

My mouth felt wet, and I realized someone's lips were pressed to mine, their tongue making its way inside. A spark of energy shot through my body as the Orgie in his mouth transferred to mine. Then, there was a third mouth, and hands on my stomach. Or maybe my stomach was the only place there weren't hands.

It didn't matter. This was a celebration. Renegayd had changed the world.

Chapter 7

Forging the Scales

My chest felt hot. As I sat up, the hand splayed across it slid off and flopped against its owner, who lay next to me at the top of the bed. Somehow, I'd made it back to my room.

"Wha!" I jumped as a foot emerged from the tangled sheets next to me. Its owner sprawled across the bottom of the bed.

Careful not to make another noise, I examined the room for any other guests. Just the three of us and the *Wizard of Oz* poster. This was B26, room 314. My mind was amazingly clear. Thank God for Orgie.

I extracted myself from the bed and tiptoed to the bathroom by the front door. A piece of paper lay in front of the door, slipped into my room from the hallway.

> *Yo, I'm standing outside your door. Sounds like you're having a good time. Glad you get over things so fast. Jesus,*

the whole floor can hear you :) We're still on for Brunhilda's at 10:30. Rainbows, sunshine, and all that shit. See you there.

"Shit." Who left this? It had to be Brun-Brun. My face flushed with heat, imagining him standing outside my room listening. *Rainbows, sunshine, and all that shit*—that didn't sound like him.

I examined the room.

A lot had happened since going with Brun-Brun to see the queen's sister. This was the second time I'd seen my bed, and there were two men sleeping in it—neither of whom was with me the first time I saw it. Circumstances are extenuating, I told myself, but I could control my hormones a bit more. Noted.

The last thing I wanted was to stir my guests. There was nothing in my room I cared about, except my Spectrum Guide, and the clock next to my guide read 10:30 a.m. I was late. Imagining Brun-Brun waiting made me squirm; so, I grabbed my Spectrum Guide, peed without flushing to avoid the noise, and left. This place is about doing whatever the hell you want. I'd certainly taken that to heart.

Brunhilda's, it turned out, was the most popular brunch spot in the city. Across the street from Pansy's Pub-erty, a chalkboard sign at the entrance announced, "All You Can Take Orgies." That was the last thing I wanted.

"There you are!"

Benj and Shǎnguang waved from a table outside the crowded brunch spot, but it was the rainbow-haired girl who popped out of her seat to welcome me.

"Yo." She fist-bumped me, and I remembered our brief meeting. "You okay? Seem a little zombified."

"Uh. Haha." I sat down, relieved and a little disappointed Brun-Brun wasn't here. "Honestly? I don't remember much from last night... *like* saying I'd meet you here. Sorry!"

Benj gave me a hearty slap on the shoulder and tilted his shock-yellow drink toward me.

"You need a drink. Hair of the werewolf," he said.

I smiled. "The last thing I need is a drink."

"You and that guy were up all night!" the girl said. "I came by at like two and heard you. *Everyone* heard you."

I didn't say anything. No need to correct her.

"More than one?" Shǎnguāng looked at me and then at Benj, laughing.

Benj's chair wobbled beneath his immense body as he howled.

"Umm," I stuttered.

"I'm Adele, remember me?" She said before taking a bite. "'M jus' kidding."

"Sorry about yer fight with Brun-Brun," Benj said.

"And sorry we're not Brun-Brun," Shǎnguāng added. Adele kicked him under the table. "Ow!"

"You can't do that to people you don't know!" Adele said. "Shǎng's an Empath. Code for nosy asshole."

"I can't hear anything you don't want me to," Shǎng said. "And I know him! Met last night."

"It's fine. I need to apologize to him. I lost it a little."

"What were you two fightin' about, anyway?" Benj asked.

"Something stupid." *Like whether or not to kill the queen. You know, silly stuff like that.* I waited for Shăng to react, but this must be on the list of things I didn't want to share.

"I know what'll cheer you up," Benj said.

"Finally!" Shăng clapped his hands and squeezed Benj's bicep in glee. "He wouldn't tell us anything until you got here."

"So," Benj started. "I met with the queen this morning. Told her about our conversation last night. Shăng, can you share it? Better than me tryin' to explain."

Adele grabbed my hand and explained, "He can share memories between people."

Shăng nodded, and without buildup or warning everything fell away. My body stayed put, but my vision flew skyward along with our connected brunch table. We hovered a moment in the pure, sapphire sky before plummeting into another scene.

The queen's voice was familiar. "It was a complete success. All over Facebook, Twitter, RenRen. Every major news outlet in the world is talking about Renegayd. They're saying the LGBT community demands to be heard!"

Benj's memory projected onto the backs of my eyelids, so his conversation with the queen seemed like my own.

"Not a *complete* success," Benj said. "There were deaths. Self-defense, but we came out of nowhere stormin' world capitols to defame them. Might've thought we were tryin' to blow 'em up."

"Oh, Benj," she condescended. "I saw the replays. They fired first, and we used our little advantages to fight back."

"Could say we instigated," he replied.

"Is that what people are saying?" She seemed bothered not by the deaths, but by the idea that they were unpopular. "That won't do, will it?"

"Attention might be worth it, but it's hard to say, to balance the equation. Last night I was talkin' with Sam, the Blank Canvas, and he was explainin' that everything we do should be calculated. The good it will do, weighed against the bad."

The queen tapped her long fingernails on the throne, smiling. "What a fantastic mind he must have," she said. The irony that all of this was her idea was lost on Benj. "And what are you suggesting?"

"An advisory council. Somethin' to let everyone know you care about collateral damage. Somethin' to help balance the scales. Prove what we're doing is worth it."

"You thought of this all by your lonesome?" she said.

"A group of us."

That seemed to make her more upset. She kept drumming her fingernails and took a deep breath. "Lots of people upset about yesterday…" she said to herself. "The people want it. The people get it!"

"Wait. Just like that?" Benj said.

"On one condition. I want that boy on it. Brun-Brun's boy toy. Sounds like he has some good ideas. I think he's got the right… disposition."

The way she said it—looking straight at me, choosing her words—made me feel like it was meant for me, at Brunhilda's, but she'd spoken to Benj hours ago.

"Of course!" replied Benj.

Could she know I would see this? The queen was a Blank Canvas, which meant nothing to me except what I'd been told over and over. Anything was possible.

The scene rocketed away as I flew into the sky, rejoining the floating table before we all plunged back down to brunch.

"Way to go, Benj!" Adele cheered. "So, it's happening?"

"It's happenin'," he confirmed. "And wonder boy Sam here's the star!"

"Why?" I asked.

"You heard it. Said you have a knack for this. Care about yer old world. I love it. All the equation-balancin' stuff was yer idea anyway."

False. And the stuff about me caring for my world wasn't a lie, but it didn't feel like the truth either. I cared about the world just enough to run back and pretend this one didn't exist.

"So when do we start?" Shǎng asked.

"Right now," answered Benj. "The queen's plannin' to follow yesterday's mission with an official announcement today. *And*, she's invited her advisory council"—Benj's hands gestured around our table as Shǎng dripped ketchup in his lap—"to have a front-row seat."

Adele squealed, "Eee! The queen wants us to be there while we're announced to the world?"

The whole table took pause. "Wouldn't have picked you for a fan girl," I said.

She glared back.

"But what are we doing?" Shǎng cut in while smearing the sauce with a napkin. "I mean, what are we *advising*?"

"This is a big deal," Benj became serious. "It isn't about doin' what's right. It's about what's least wrong. Gays in yer world are bein' hurt. They're killin' themselves. Renegayd'll force change, and we're gonna be at the center of it."

"One wrong—to prevent two…" Adele started. "Makes it right? It's not that simple."

"That's why we're here," I said, catching the excitement. "To debate that. To scrutinize and make sure the equation winds up on the side of good."

"What will we call ourselves?" Shǎng asked.

"The Justice League," Adele laughed.

"The Scales," Benj said. "Scales of Justice."

I did have a hair of the werewolf before the Scales of Justice parted for the first time. With the few hours before the queen's announcement, I wanted to share the news with Brun-Brun. To apologize. Besides, this would let me stay close to the queen and keep things from getting out of hand.

I checked Pansy's Pub-crty first. Then, the store across the Transpo Hub; I roamed a few floors of the Ivory Tower but failed at retracing our path to Enyo's faux mirror. Brun-Brun had spent his entire life in a city I'd just discovered. I didn't even know where to start.

Chapter 8

Sugar and Cinnamon

"We demand Perfect Equality globally. The LGBT community is through asking for ordination, and no normalcy—no sameness—will end our struggle. We demand liberation, and we reject that it comes in stages. Some see a gay, white man on TV and shout 'Progress!' Some see rights permitting marriage conformity and shout 'Equality!' We do not. We see that we're homeless and hungry, sick and bullied, underpaid, and suicidal. Renegayd is breaking that white picket prison and bringing back the revolution.

"*Smash the Church! Smash the State! We will bring an end to hate!* Seventy-nine countries may criminalize our community's existence, but that will change. It will change, because this time, the oppressed wield the power. To our gay, lesbian, bi, trans, and queer family. Renegayd is for you. If you're scared, bullied, or imprisoned, my world is open to you. Join us. Fight injustice. Be empowered."

The world changed to the sound of Mozart's Symphony No. 40 in G minor. It might have been possible for the world's governments to write off Renegayd's graffiti coming out, bury it as a bad dream. The queen was making sure that didn't happen. Her Scales of Justice packed into the control room with many others to witness the first global media hack. Benj, Adele, Shǎnguāng, and I sat behind the controller, who occupied the triangular room's point behind a panel of pulsing colors, dials, and switches that transmitted the queen's audio and visual feed from this world to the other.

The queen stood behind the glass window to our right, staring down the little red light of a single camera while she changed the world. She was the star of the show, but I was captivated by the unsung hero, the magic that made the whole thing work. Hack, a mousy, pimpled boy behind the window to our left. His Spectrum ability allowed him to control technology—through dance. He wasn't a gifted dancer, nor is Mozart made for dancing, but with every hip thrust, jazz hand, or raising of the roof, he co-opted servers and radio towers.

Hack ensured the queen's announcement wasn't just geographically global. It was everywhere. He hijacked every social newsfeed, staged a homepage takeover of media outlets from Al Jazeera to CNN to BBC, and overpowered every AM and FM frequency on Earth.

"Our cause—global LGBT liberation—is no passing fad. We're pickin' up the book on civil rights and flipping to the end of our chapter. No more waiting for a trickle to erode the mountain of hate. There will be liberation, because we demand it. Our path, though, can still be chosen. These demands, radical may they be in transformation, only require the most basic human dignity. If this makes your heart sing, then Honeycakes, we've got a place for you! When this transmission ends, Renegayd will hold recruitment in every gayborhood in the world. From SoHo, to Le Marais, to the Castro, to Schöneberg and beyond. Renegayd's first global recruitment event is today! Go to Renegayd.lgbt for a city near you!"

Benj tapped Shǎnguāng on the shoulder, and they shared a concerned look.

"Which brings me to the rest of you fuckers: the bullies, abusers, and imprisoners. You're no longer on the wrong side of history; you're on the wrong side of power. This fairy's pissed off, and I'm comin' for you."

The queen raised her fist to the camera, displaying rainbow fingernails, before the transmission ended.

Cheers erupted in the control room, and the queen blew a kiss our way. This was much more coordinated than I'd imagined. It felt like even in those few minutes we made progress, like the momentum we were building was good.

The controller held down a button and spoke. "Killed it, Queeny."

"Booyah bitches!" She tapped the glass, looking through our control room to the other wall of the triangle. "Hack, you wonderful darling. Brilliant! Just brilliant!"

Hack blushed and nodded, then pushed his glasses back onto his nose. He'd danced himself into a sweat.

"We need to talk about this recruitin' campaign," said Benj. "This really a good idea?"

"I was inspired!" the queen replied.

"You had a website," Benj refuted. "You fired up the opposition and told 'em right where we'll be to voice complaints. It's dangerous."

"Womp womp. Is this what you want your Scales of Justice to be?" Benj wagged his finger at the queen. "Fine!" she continued. "Why don't you four come with me to the Transpo Hub? I'll introduce you. That way I can't pull any more fast ones without your approval. Fair?"

Benj smiled. She was hard to resist.

"Well? You ready?" she asked.

"Let's do it," Adele cheered.

The queen cocked her wand. "Toodles!" With a lazy twist of her wrist, a blast of glitter shot from her wand straight through the window into my face. I inhaled a mouthful.

Thunderous applause alerted me to the sudden appearance of an audience to my choking on glitter. We were on a stage, beneath the Transpo Hub arch, in front of people all entertained by my unceremonious entrance.

"He swallowed," the queen quipped, and then shushed the crowd. "Renegayd! You heard it! We're out and proud! It's time to find us some allies. This is a recruitment mission. Renegayd will be a force for good in *both* worlds! Bring back anyone who needs our protection. My Ivory Tower is home to those who need it."

Benj met the queen's gaze.

"*And* I want to introduce y'all to some special folks. Our quest may be righteous, but our rainbow's in grey skies. These people—the Scales of Justice—will be our measuring stick, ensuring we don't misstep, making our actions feel—oh! so!

good!" Renegayd cheered as the queen touched herself. Then she motioned to me. "Sam DeSalvo will enlighten us with a few words."

Benj stabbed his hand forward to usher me up. Everyone stared, and for no reason, I was center stage.

"Just, uh, be careful. We made at least as many people angry as we made happy."

The queen gave an animated, grinning nod—histrionic agreement blessing anything I said—except I had nothing else to say. The great Scales of Justice reveal reduced to white noise from the crowd: awkward shuffling, a sneeze. The queen finally aborted my pregnant pause.

"The Scales of Justice, everyone!" She opened her hands and spun around to face the doors inside the Transpo Hub. "Let's go! Through the portals! Spread the love!"

Our stage became a surf break as Renegayd surged and barreled into every Transpo Hub closet door chanting, "Smash the Church! Smash the State! We will bring an end to hate!"

The queen ran to the front of the stage.

"*RENEGAYD*!" She pointed her wand to the sky. "Change the world!"

And as she said *world*, streams of glitter gushed above the crowd, so thick that it wasn't the sun shining down, but its dazzling reflection shading faces in yellows, purples, greens, and blues.

The queen draped her arms around Adele and me, admiring her ocean of followers. Who knows how long she'd waited for this. I wanted to ask about Brun-Brun—to see if she knew where he was—but it would have to wait. Instead, I mimicked what I thought someone on her Scales of Justice would say.

"We'll make good," I tried.

"Good and evil," the queen whispered, "are a matter of perspective. The secret's finding the angle that blocks out the other side. Remember that."

When I looked to respond, there was a pile of glitter where the queen had stood, arms no longer on my shoulder but her weight remaining.

Adele leaned over the opposite side of the stage, waving at people as they disappeared into closet doors. She considered this the most significant day in LGBT history, and since I'd taken the Spectrum test, the closet doors would work for me. We had to experience it firsthand.

*****

The first thing I noticed was the smell of sugar and cinnamon. With one foot in the Transpo Hub, my senses somersaulted as my other fell beyond the closet portal's threshold.

If there was one place to ease the transition between gay fantasyland and harsh reality, it was Hot Cookie. Though I'd never been behind the counter, my familiarity with the tiny shop's customer-side helped in orienting where I was in the Castro. The two employees appeared not to notice the thirty or forty people pouring out of their storage closet. They were too busy working the miniature counter, where a line of people clamored to get their hands around phallic-shaped macaroons. Maybe an Empath eased their apprehension, or maybe we weren't quite strange enough to merit attention.

I felt as though this was my first day as a full person. Purpose-driven, part of something—returning home to share Renegayd's intoxicating rebirth, a message of Perfect Equality, of liberation. Someone handed me a stack of fliers reading, "Come Out, Come Out, Wherever You Are!"

"Let's get recruiting!"

We poured into the street with fellow Renegayd members to find the Castro mid-celebration. It was clear the queen's message had indeed reached the world. I could imagine a more mixed reaction elsewhere, but in the Bay a public fight for equality was a reason to party.

Only a few token protestors showed the diversity of hate we were up against:

Ex-gays: *Not Gay! Ex-gay, post-gay and proud. Get over it!*

Un-naturals: *Identical Twins. One Gay. One Not. Nobody born gay.*

Religious: *Leviticus 20.*

People mocked and danced around the protestors, and amidst the revelry I spotted a boy holding his mom's coat with a sign reading, *God H8S Fags* strapped to his back. He looked clueless, and I wondered if he could read the sign let alone understand it. His mother pointed straight at me and shouted: "Homosexuality's a behavior. Not a civil right. Protect our children! Restore marriage."

"Is that woman crying?" Adele asked.

She was, and she continued. "Wake up Christians! God was not wrong. God's word is truth, and *God* says marriage is between a man and a woman. All these people saying they're Christians... you're celebrating? Do we read the same bible?! Wake up! Jesus died for you, and you're spitting in his face!"

Someone shouting my name pushed my attention back to the sidewalk and the wider party.

"Sam? What the fuck!" Before processing who was talking he had leaped into my arms and wrapped his legs around me. "Where the fuck have you been?"

"Jacob! It's been forever!" I said, unsure of how much time had passed here since my succubus visit.

"Sooo? How was hot Frenchie?"

"Sort of sucked."

"Not bad for a rebound! That. Night. Was. Epic! Where'd you go? I've been texting you!"

"Yeah, sorry. I don't know where to start."

"This is soo cray, right?" He said, not knowing the half of it.

Adele shoved a flier between us. "Name's Adele. Thanks for the intro, Sam." Jacob pounded her fist. "We're recruiting for Renegayd. Have you heard about us?"

Jacob did a double take. "You? Wait, you're recruiting for Renegayd?"

"Sounds like you've heard," Adele continued.

"Whole damn world has! We came down to see if it was real!" Jacob turned around. "Guys! My friend is recruiting for Renegayd!"

Several people pushed through the crowd to surround us, all dying to learn more.

"Why didn't you tell me about this?" Jacob asked while Adele explained to the larger group. "How long has all this been going on?"

"You're not going to believe me. That night with the French guy, I went through some kind of portal. There's like a whole fantasy world on the other side of this place. I swear. I teleported back through Hot Cookie's back closet." Jacob looked blank. "You know how Hogwarts is for wizards, but it connects to the real world?"

"Hyea," he said.

"This is like the gay version of that, except instead of wizards there's regular people, like us."

"Yeah?"

A flash of heat blasted up beside us, followed by ferocious applause.

"I'm a Flamer," Adele explained to the group. "You could be one too. It all depends on your Spectrum results."

A tiny fire snake slithered between her fingers.

"You're fucking serious?" Jacob squealed. "HOLY FUCKING SHIT! This is amazing! This is like X-Men, but instead of mutant equality, it's gay. Take me. Wait, what's your power? Are you Iceman or Jean Grey? I wanna be Jean Grey! You've gotta show me. You'll take me there, right?"

The group we'd attracted blocked the street, all crowding around to hear more and watch Adele do flame tricks.

"Yeah! I can take you there. That's why we're here. Recruiting members to fight for gay liberation. California *just* got marriage equality, and we're way ahead of other states, other countries! It's moving too slowly. We're trying to speed things up."

"I'm in. You had me at Hogwarts for gays. Oh God." Jacob grabbed my arm. "You had sex with a wizard, didn't you? That Frenchie? I want to have sex with Dumbledore!"

"We need all the help we can get."

He squealed again.

A piercing horn broke up the crowd that had spilled into the street, and everyone parted to let three black Hummers roll down Castro Street. The third stopped in front of us, while the other two continued down Castro. A white flag with *Mission Morality* hastily painted on it draped out from a window, and a man popped out of the sunroof holding a megaphone.

"Faggots and sinners! Listen up! Thank you for getting together to make this easy."

The man pulled his other arm out of the sunroom, pointed a machine gun in the air, and fired above his head. Screams spread down Castro as shots fired from the other two Humvees.

"For our children!"

The windows rolled down, revealing more maniacs all pointing weapons at the crowd. It no longer mattered what the man was saying; he moved his weapon from the sky to the sidewalk across the street from us.

Pop-pop-pop.

I grabbed Jacob's hand.

"Infesting rathole neighborhoods—we won't tolerate abomination anymore!"

Pop-pop-pop and screams.

Shouting for Adele, I sprinted toward Hot Cookie. "Adele! Come on!"

She was squared up to the Humvee, her fire snake spinning around itself. The backseat window rolled down, and I shoved Jacob toward Hot Cookie to run for Adele. A shirtless lunatic swung out of the vehicle with a machine gun aimed at Adele as she wound up to pitch her fireball.

Pop-pop-pop.

A pale blue monolith grew out of the concrete in front of my friend. Someone beat me to her, tackling her to the ground behind the inexplicable statue. Adele and her savior rolled beneath the Castro Theater ticket booth, as her fireball engulfed the left side of the Humvee.

"ADELE! Shit! Adele! Are you okay?"

An old man lay next to her, glasses bent out of shape.

"We're alright, sonny," the man said between gasping breaths. "Get up and defend your home."

"THANK YOU!" Adele put one of her arms around the grey man, hugging him as they lay on the ground.

"We've got to get out of here!" I screamed. "Back to the closet!"

A deafening thunderclap reverberated over the scattered gunfire, and an explosion billowed from a few doors down. Heat poured over us. People hurtled through the glass wall of the corner bus stop, replacing the line of cookiemongers with twisted metal and bloodied bodies. Hot Cookie was gone.

"The closet!" Adele shouted.

"JACOB!"

I'd dragged him right to Hot Cookie's doorstep. The *pop-pop-pop* continued, and I approached the wreckage shouting for my friend.

"Sam!"

Jacob limped across the street back towards the rubble the blast had launched him from. His right leg, arm, and side of his face were ruined, skin bloodied and blistered where it wasn't absent. Adele's flames were extinguished, and the gunner on our side of the street draped half out of the passenger window, dead.

The man at the top of the vehicle was shooting the opposite side of the street.

"Are you okay?" I asked, to which Jacob groaned as I put his arm around him.

The Castro was under attack. Bombs erupted by each of the three Humvees. Hot Cookie, Eighteenth and Castro, and Twenty-Second.

"Penis," Jacob grunted, and I saw what he meant. We hobbled straight for it.

The statue that had saved Adele's life was a massive, veiny dick made of cerulean concrete that grew straight out of the ground. A second penis sheltered Adele and the old man beneath Castro Theater's neon.

"The closet's gone!" Adele yelled to us from behind her cock-cover.

"Keep your wits," said the old man. "The natural portal's still here."

"That's right! It's at Eighteenth and Castro," I remembered.

"Get me my cane."

If we could make it to the corner, the pole next to Harvey's could take us back. Jacob and I shuffled from our penis to theirs and squeezed up against the shaft for protection.

The old man grabbed his cane and waddled out from behind the penis statue. With a cheeky smile he faced the Humvee, lifted his cane, and smacked it against the ground. The pavement quaked, and another statue grew beneath the Humvee. This one was at least three times the size of the first two, and as the erection grew, it caught the left side of the vehicle, lifting it off the ground until it tipped on its side.

Two more times, the man tapped his cane, unleashing a penile offensive on the two remaining vehicles. With three taps and three stone erections, the man had stopped the *pop-pop-pop*.

"Alright!" shouted Adele, and she ran for the old man.

"NOT YET," he shouted back.

His cane slammed the ground over and over, until each Humvee was imprisoned by a circle of blue boners. It looked safe, but we waited until he nodded. It was over. Mission Morality was imprisoned or dead. We didn't need to run to the portal at the pole. Instead, we could take in the destruction.

No music. No laughing. Nothing but distant sirens and muffled cries from people who'd been in the wrong place at the wrong time. The world had known Renegayd for one day. How had they organized so quickly?

A white piece of fabric blew in the breeze toward Eighteenth.

"Adele, help me." I motioned to Jacob.

"What are you doing?" She asked, accepting his weight. "Are you trying to get yourself killed?"

I ran down the street and trapped the half-burned piece of fabric under my foot. Looking back at my friends I realized how lucky we were. Even with Jacob wounded, supported by Adele who would be dead were it not for the old man's bizarre Spectrum ability, we were alive.

"They were here because of us," I said, showing the Mission Morality flag to Adele and shouldering Jacob's weight. "I have to get him through the portal. Help the others."

"Sam, this isn't our fault."

"Just help them, please."

Clutching the Mission Morality flag, Jacob and I hobbled to

the natural portal. Someone would be able to help him, but there were many beyond the Spectrum's reach. The queen had said it was easy when things were black and white—good and evil. This made things easy. The Scales of Justice had work to do.

Chapter 9

Healing

I'd returned through the portal shouting for help that was already prepared. The queen knew about the attack, and the whole city rallied to care for the wounded coming back through the portal. Dionysia took Jacob to the medical ward herself repeating that the most helpful thing I could do was prepare for an immediate Scales of Justice meeting. My refusal withered against her resolve, and as the retina scanner opened the door to my room, I felt the fullness of my exhaustion, her wisdom. Staring at my feet in the shower, water washed dried blood, soot and filth down the drain.

Mission Morality affirmed everything we stood for. The fear felt in the Castro was mixed with pride in having a say in what we did next. Renegayd was ablaze with purpose. Our next move would shape both worlds.

I wrapped a towel around my waste, stepped out of the shower, and into my room. A shadow in the corner spurred energy I thought Mission Morality had sapped.

"Brun-Brun?" The figure stepped out of the shadows, and I stopped short of running into Enyo's arms. Instead, I got dressed, resigned to the intrusion. "I'm not in the mood."

"You look horrible," she said.

"What are you doing here? Come to feed me more bullshit?"

Enyo looked upset. "You call Mission Morality bullshit?"

"Serious shit. Forgive me for not applauding your sneaking in the shadows. *Really* helping the cause. You keep doing that; meanwhile we're having the first meeting of the Scales to try to do something about it."

"Renegayd created Mission Morality!"

"Reactions to what we do will show how far we need to go," I said. "Those people didn't suddenly hate us. They're just coming to the surface."

"That's what you think?"

"Look, I'm trying to do the right thing. You're not doing anything." I sighed.

"Fine." She leaned closer. "I wanted to ask if you've seen Brun-Brun."

"You haven't seen him? I wanted to invite him to our meeting."

"Shit," Enyo disengaged. "He's gone."

"What do you mean? Where does he live?"

There was a loud knock on the door, and then Adele shouted through it, "Yo! You in there?"

I tried to be quiet. I wasn't leaving without Enyo telling me what she knew.

"Hellllo!"

"Uh. Gimme a minute!" I tried.

"What are you doing in there? I want to ask you something."

"Please," I whispered to Enyo. "If you know something, you have to tell me."

"Someone in there with you?" Adele asked, and the handle rattled. "Christ, Sam! Here I was all worried about you.... Sorry, whoever-you-are! Need to borrow him for a minute! Scales of Justice business!"

"You think Brun-Brun's the first?" Enyo said. "You must have noticed."

"Where is he? Tell me, or I'll tell everyone about you. The queen is looking for you anyway."

"I don't know where he is," Enyo snapped. "I guess your ignorance shouldn't surprise me. You've ignored everything."

"What do you mean?"

"Follow the missing people," she said.

"SAM!" Adele shouted.

"Where is he?" I tried again.

"You're asking the wrong sibling." Enyo motioned for me to leave.

I opened the door a crack and slipped through, Enyo's warning seeping into me just like it had the first time we'd met.

"Who's in there?" Adele teased, trying to peek past me. "Thought you might want some company, but apparently that's taken care of. Come on—let's check on your friend."

I tried to laugh, but it sounded like I felt: fake. Spectrum graduate without an ability, foreigner to this world, scheming to use the Scales of Justice to *follow the missing people*. Enyo hadn't changed my mind, but she had made me suspicious.

Adele led the way to the medical ward, explaining what she'd wanted to discuss as we walked. "I'm having a crisis of conscience. I think we're both unconvinced by the whole Renegayd thing. The queen created the Scales of Justice after one meeting with Benj? Isn't that a bit rash?"

"Is it possible for a group of people to all lose their minds together?" I said.

"Ha!" Adele gave me a side hug while we walked.

"The queen's using the Scales to keep an eye on dissent. We're the canary in the coal mine, making sure she doesn't do something so unpopular she loses her followers."

Adele nodded. "So where's that leave us? Is there any chance to squeeze some good out of this?"

I paused, wondering how much to divulge. "I feel like there's something else going on behind the scenes."

"What do you mean?" she asked.

"I don't know. Brun-Brun is gone, and I think the queen might have something to do with it."

"Haven't we got bigger problems than your boyfriend running off?"

"I'm serious. It feels like something bad may have happened."

"Yeah, we just saw it happening." Adele pressed a button on the elevator. "I'm focused on the Scales. I think Benj is Queen-loyal to the core, and I don't see Shǎng disagreeing with him. I don't know what's going to happen, but if we can't manage to direct all this to good, then I want out."

"Me too. It feels hopeless. Can four people really," I searched for the right words, "Control the queen?"

"Tall order. We can at least tell each other everything. Promise?"

We pounded in agreement. Hiding Enyo wasn't a great start.

The entrance to the medical ward had a big QUIET PLEASE sign above the entrance. Adele took a deep breath and smiled as we approached, my opposite reaction to entering what could only be a gruesome scene after the attack.

"What are you smiling at?" I asked.

"We may both be Transplants, but sometimes I forget how green you still are."

The lack of gemstone-fairies made opening the medical ward door comparably unremarkable, but stepping onto the soft dirt on the other side met expectations. I almost turned around.

"Is this—?"

Adele pushed me in. "The medical ward, yup."

Somehow, this floor in the Ivory Tower contained a massive farm. Rows of mounded dirt striated the landscape, and grow lights hung from the ceiling, their heat spreading the scent of manure. The walls didn't fit the scene, plain, like the hallway, except for cabana-like rooms extending out from the main farmland. A few people tended the farm, but most were in the private cabanas with the patients, identifiable by large signs over each semi-private room that read "Patient #1" "Patient #2" and so on out of view.

A scarecrow-like woman approached. She put her finger to her lips.

Adele whispered, "Jacob."

"Patient #42," the woman replied. "You're just in time."

The woman pulled a piece of straw from her shirt pocket, put it in her mouth, and led us down a row of mounded dirt. Occasional sprigs broke the surface, each one labeled with a miniature garden sign.

I felt all the questions I'd trained away pop back up, and I could barely hold back when our spindly farmhand knelt over a specific crop labeled "Patient #42." She surveyed the sprig before plunging her hand into the red dirt, tipping the sign as she uprooted a yellow and green bulb. The bulb blossomed with a tiny squeak. Its pedals, long and sharp, undulated in the woman's hand while she continued down the row towards room forty-two.

Up a single stair, out of the dirt, lay Jacob still burned and untended on a cot.

"Jacob!"

"Hey." His face scrunched in pain. "Not quite what I imagined."

The farmhand took charge of the room, swinging a tray over the bed and sitting on a chair at his bedside.

"Have you fixed in a jiffy. Well, this guy'll be doing the fixin'." She plopped the yellow-green crop on the tray. "These two came to see you. Don't have to let them stay, though. It can be awkward. Choice is yours."

Jacob's whole right side was burned. His scorched arm and leg were exposed, and he still wore the singed clothes from the Castro. He shifted on top of the still-made bed and cringed.

"It's fine whatever. Just do it."

The farmer removed the straw from her mouth, leaned over the metal tray, and spit on the chartreuse bulb.

"Eeeee!" It quivered, and the crop jumped up to stand, somehow balanced on its thin pedals.

"Ey ya. Heal this one here. Ya hear?"

"Eeeee!" Tiny green eyes opened above the crop's fleshy

middle, which puckered in and palpitated as it spoke in high-pitched squeaks. "Heeee's hurt."

"I know he's hurt!" The woman laughed. "You need to help him!"

"Ooooh."

"Right here," the woman pointed to Jacob arm. "And here." His face. "And his leg too."

"Ooooh. That's not all."

"What do you mean that's not all?"

The little creature hopped with great effort onto Jacob's chest and pointed one pedal straight down.

"Heerre too."

"Oh, that's okay. You don't need to fix that."

"Huh? But—."

"Just what I showed you please."

"Pleeease!" the crop urged.

The woman looked over her shoulder, embarrassed. "Got a stubborn one. Always stubborn with the Transplants." She turned back to the crop. "Fine. Go for it."

"Okay! Bye bye!" The crop looked at the farmer, eyes widening.

"Bye bye now," she said, and the crop lay down on Jacob's chest.

Its pedals stopped moving. As if dried in the sun, the perky bulb dulled to brown and wilted, shriveling to a quarter-sized raisin with brittle pedals that broke off when the woman picked it up and offered it to Jacob.

"Alright! Down the hatch then."

Jacob furrowed his brow, and then yelped in pain. "You want me to eat that?"

"Or, get infected and probably die. Who knows?"

"Aren't you a doctor?" Jacob asked.

"I look like a doctor to you?"

"It's okay," Adele said, and I nodded in agreement.

Jacob took the dead snack and managed to swallow it whole. "How do you feel?" The farmer asked.

"Tastes gross, but—" he stopped talking to look at his arm.

Jacob's blisters bubbled and flattened. The open wounds closed up, transforming into yellow-green skin, and the surrounding redness faded. His leg and face healed the same, leaving a tidy yellow-green residue in place of ruin.

"Sorry about the next bit. Maybe it'll help. Who knows."

"I—." He fidgeted, not in physical pain but struggling against something. "It's just… I try to block this out. What's happening?" His new cheek scrunched as he sniffled. "I'm happy now. Why—." He struggled against something fighting inside him, and then all at once he blurted out: "They called me a faggot in middle school."

"What's going on?" I asked, but the farmer just nodded as Jacob continued.

"The big moments like that hurt, but the little ones always took me by surprise. Mocking behind my back, flapping their hands—making fun of me. A stranger on a bus asked if I was gay seconds after meeting. I didn't even know yet!"

Somehow the crop forced this story out of Jacob, along with the pain that came from telling it.

"These jerks just kept picking. Jumped me after PE—they almost killed me! But, when my parents asked why it happened I said I didn't know. I couldn't tell them it was because they thought I was gay, that *I* thought I was gay. So, they got away with it, and I went farther in the closet. It took ten years from then until I came out. Just wasted."

"There there. All done?" The farmer sat up. "Got a real kicker! You're all set."

I couldn't hold back anymore. "Wait! What the hell happened? Jacob, are you okay?"

He sat up, healed.

"I'm a Remedy," the farmer said. "My crops heal people—obviously."

"What about... that. Was all that necessary?"

"He's healed ain't he?"

"But what's with that story?"

"Little fella thought he could heal his heart. Lot harder than that unfortunately, but who knows. Maybe it helps."

Jacob sat up.

"I'm Sorry," Jacob started. "I can't—."

"It's fine." I cut him off. He didn't need to relive what I already understood.

"Renegayd's here to make sure nobody else goes through that. Look, Adele and I are part of this thing called the Scales of Justice. We're about to meet for the first time, but after Mission Morality and the attack... we can't do this alone. You should come."

"And do what?" he asked.

"We don't know yet, but maybe you can help us find the good in all this."

"Or misery might just love company," Adele added.

Jacob took a minute to touch the new skin on his arm and

leg. He balled his fist, reached above his head, and then looked out at the farmhand who was already walking back down the rows of dirt.

"Thank you!" he shouted.

"Shhhh!" she replied, genuinely distraught by his outburst.

"This place gets weirder and weirder." Jacob gave a big goofy grin. "Alright. I mean fuck it, of course I'll join you!"

Chapter 10

Utility Positive

The glass elevator took us above the clouds to the room the queen had provided for Scales of Justice use, and at the elevator ding, the weight of what we were doing descended, at least for me. Adele opened the door to our room, and with her hand over her mouth, ran across it chanting, "Lou. Lou. Lou."

A complicated handshake ended with boisterous laughter, and Adele introduced her friend, a short woman with a ponytail sticking out the back of a ball cap, as our sixth and final member.

"Guess I'm free to advise the queen in a secret group." Lou waved to Jacob and I. "This place is insane!"

There were a few minutes of summer camp mingling, as Lou and Jacob met the others. No debate, no utility-of-lives, just people looking for someone to share a pudding cup. Benj and Shăng thought it balanced things to have our friends join. They knew their relationship gave them an unfair advantage, but this gave us equal footing.

Benj reeled us back to reality. "Everyone! We gotta get started. Plans to make! Worlds to change!"

The room quieted, and we pulled up a circle of chairs in the middle of the room. It was awkward, silent. Everyone deferred to Benj, but he looked at me.

"Well?" Benj said. "The queen appointed you our leader."

I tried to detect any jealousy, but Benj looked at Shǎng, who smiled and nodded.

"Okay. First thing is we're all equal. Everyone gets a chance to speak, and we hear each other out." The room nodded, providing a fragment of confidence for me to continue. "So, uh, yeah this is the first meeting of the Scales of Justice!"

Lou clapped a few times and then spoke up. "Look, we're all wondering the same thing. Did Renegayd create Mission Morality? Their attacks on our recruitment pretty much answer that."

"Wait?" I interrupted. "There were multiple attacks?"

"Yeah. Where've you been the past few hours?" Lou replied.

"We were a little busy getting shot at in the Castro," Jacob defended.

"You and everyone else," Lou said. "Castro and three other recruitment sites. All by people claiming to be part of this, Mission Morality. News says they used message boards to plan it."

"But Renegayd came out yesterday!" Adele replied.

"These people didn't start hatin' gays yesterday," Brun-Brun said. "We riled 'em up. If a few people and some message boards managed four attacks. We should think about what happens when they expand."

"Expand?" Jacob sounded worried.

"Wouldn't give em'selves a name if they didn't plan on usin' it," Benj replied.

"They'll be celebrated," Adele added. "This was a recruitment of their own."

"Mission Morality exists," Shǎng said flatly. "Does it matter how they came to be?"

"I think it does," said Adele. "If something as horrible as Mission Morality can be created by our actions, we need to take that into account. That's what we're here to do, right? Balance the good and the bad."

"We need something to write on," I said.

A chalkboard appeared on the wall next to us, and Jacob squealed. He looked straight at me and whispered, "*the Room of Requirement.*" Nobody else batted an eye, too steeped in this place to be fazed by the simple trick.

"I need a magic wand," Jacob tried, but nothing happened. "How about a pet monkey." Still nothing.

"Piece of chalk," Benj said, and one appeared in his outstretched hand. "Be reasonable."

"Glass of water?"

Sure enough, a cup appeared in the air and fell, before he could grab it, straight into Jacob's lap. He grinned, more amazed than embarrassed. Lou moved to the chalkboard and wrote "GOOD" and "BAD" with a vertical line between them. She then listed a few things on each side.

Good: Equality.
Bad: Death. Mission Morality?

"Not looking great for us." Lou joked.

"Hold up," Shǎng said. "It's not that simple. What about the safety people feel because someone's fighting for them? For a lot of kids, this may be the first time they've seen someone like them fighting back."

Jacob added, "Renegayd probably changed a few minds during the queen's broadcast. Millions of people saw it. It at least increased awareness about inequality."

"Mission Morality helped there, too," Benj said.

We worked through the list of good and bad until we'd filled the chalkboard. Some areas were so smeared from rewrites that it was hard to read the finished version, but by the end we had one list of simple words and another of long sentences trying to capture loose concepts. Arrows designated many of them as being both good and bad.

"So…?" Lou dangled the question during the lunch we'd materialized.

Everyone turned to me. It had been hours since I'd been anything but a member of the group, but it seemed that any time we were stuck, I'd be back to leading.

"Anyone have anything else they can think of?" I said.

"Sure. All of these can have degrees to them," Jacob said. "Like, taking over global media channels is linked to the company we hack. Hijacking a liberal tech company that agrees with our cause is a lot less harmful than hijacking conservative news talk." The others stared at him, exhausted from debating and brainstorming and wordsmithing. "You asked if we could think of anything else. All I'm saying is there's like an infinite amount of other stuff."

I walked over to the list and, right between *Good* and *Bad*, drew a big *X*.

"Here's your grey area, then," I said, happy to placate the point. "With Jacob's grey X, we can call this an all-inclusive list of the good and bad that Renegayd has done."

Everyone nodded, but so what?

A splutter of glitter poofed up between me and the rest of the Scales. It grew into a puddle and then took shape until the queen was with us.

"How are my Scales of Justice? Balancing things? Weighing good and evil?" She smiled and turned to the chalkboard. "Ohh! Look at this. Here it is right here!"

Benj replied first. "We hit a wall. No stone's unturned for how things have been goin', but we don't know what to do next."

"I've got good news then!" the queen said. "I've decided what to do next, and I've come seeking your counsel."

I wanted to say, *How dare you!* We'd been debating right and wrong for hours, and she appears from nowhere to tell us what's next? But Benj said matter of factly what I was only realizing.

"You make the plans. We'll vet 'em."

We weren't her strategists. We were the Scales of Justice, here to deliberate the utility of *her* decisions, to check and balance *her* power. Judiciary to our monarch.

She explained her plan: heightened recruitment.

"If Mission Morality is declaring itself our opposition, there'll be more people wanting to help. Polarization lets us collect all the fresh faces running from the other side. So, let's welcome them with open arms! Open the natural portals to any LGBT person who wants to join—give them the Spectrum test—grow our ranks!" She paused for our reaction, and we all looked at each other. "What? My teeth got lipstick on them?"

The queen checked her compact mirror, while I explained our reaction.

"We just spent hours discussing how polarization works both ways. Mission Morality may react."

"Hmph," she said, re-pocketing the mirror. "So, inviting endangered LGBT people into this world is bad?"

"Risky," I corrected. "We saw what happened with impromptu recruitment. We'll need to be careful, but if we can manage that," I looked at the board, "I think the utility's there."

"Me too," Jacob agreed. "Added benefit of getting some gays out of harm's way. I was in pretty bad shape, came through the portal, and look at me now!" He stood up, blushing as the group's gaze went to the wet spot where his water had spilled.

The queen applauded. "Fabulous! I've been thinking about how all this should work. We need to let the people know you were involved. That this is the right thing to do. Give it your stamp of approval! We need a piece of paper"—the room provided one—"and a pen." She handed them to me. "Write down what you told me. *The utility is there.* That sounds fantastic. Maybe a bit more to help people understand why this is right. Assume everybody's thinking what you are… and convince them."

I scrawled something close to what I remembered saying on the paper.

"There!" She snatched the paper out from under my pen. "And a little spruce up!"

Her wand transformed my illegible handwriting into calligraphy, and the title sparkled: *Utility Positive*.

"What do we do with it?" Benj asked.

"We distribute."

The queen placed her wand against the glass wall overlooking the clouds and touched the paper to the opposite end. All at once the paper was sucked up into the wand and spat out on the opposite side of the glass. As the sheet fluttered down, the wand created another copy. One after another, her wand released thousands of fliers above the clouds to rain down on the city below.

"Ya know," the queen said, "this whole Scales of Justice thing could work."

Chapter 11

Monochromatic

Why had it required transplanting to another world for me to see the grey? It must have always been there, and I'd never noticed. Like the stakes were too low, or I was too self-absorbed. Now though, the whole world was grey. Anything could be rationalized when I put my mind to it, and that made everything more difficult.

The queen was the opposite. For her, every shade was rounded to the nearest black or white. I asked her about Brun-Brun, and she got angry. Told me to concentrate on making myself useful. Blank Canvas… still blank. Her response took me by surprise, stalling me long enough for her to find an exit, but the constant dodging signaled proof of her involvement.

I couldn't shake the feeling that Brun-Brun was in trouble, but the grey kept interfering with my search for him. Recruiting had been Utility Positive—wildly successful from a numbers perspective—but Mission Morality was a shadow that seemed to grow alongside us. So my time was monopolized by utility debates, instead of finding Brun-Brun.

Renegayd and Mission Morality were opposites with diametric demands: LGBT equality or LGBT oppression. The largest difference between organizations, we told ourselves, was the Scales of Justice. We kept Renegayd on the high road while Mission Morality sank lower. We were changing the world, optimizing the queen's plans to maximize utility. Recruiting and harboring oppressed LGBT people in this world was one example of that good. Things were grey, but the Scales agreed it was healthy to condense doubt within our small group rather than burden the whole movement. Our calligraphy-adorned decisions fell from the clouds, to spread clarity on the utility of every action we took in the month since Renegayd increased recruiting.

Each member of the Scales of Justice was a crutch for the next. We kept each other going as Mission Morality drew out the world's hate. No country outright endorsed Mission Morality or Renegayd, but there were underhanded actions for both. Where Renegayd received information and tips from liberal governments; others granted Mission Morality members asylum. When Renegayd received un-solicited donations from businesses and people in support of Global Equality, Mission Morality received the same in support of the opposite.

News stations polled public support, their thermometers showing popular opinion of each organization's actions and reactions. Hate and love were never more divergent, and that in turn created more grey to be shouldered by the Scales, more doubt to be shielded from the organization.

"Do you think we'll ever *get* Perfect Equality?" I asked.

Jacob and I carried our Spectrum Guides out of the elevator onto one of many floors in the Ivory Tower dedicated to Spectrum training. Benj maintained that *believing and deciding* was the way to obtain a Spectrum power, but Jacob had already shown more promise than I had since taking his test.

"Absolutely" Jacob answered. "Why else would we be doing all this?"

"It's still worth it, but don't you feel like we're chasing a false reality. Has any discriminated group ever really reached Perfect Equality?"

Jacob stopped in the hallway, near a vibrating door.

"You don't mean that," he whispered, like we were discussing some huge subversion. "We're the ones leading this. If we don't believe it, how do we expect others to fight for it?"

"Sure yeah, I guess you're right."

"For sure," he said, continuing down the hall. "You brought me here for God sakes! For which I am eternally grateful."

He turned around, hands together, and bowed, returning to his goofy self.

Each of the closed doors we past had its sign showing a red "X," *Occupied*, letting the hallway masquerade as an elementary or middle school when class was in session. Only a few nurtured Spectrum abilities spoiled that cover: smoke billowed from the cracks around one door; another flashed different colors; and another seeped strange noises into the hall.

Jacob's Spectrum proctor had booked him a training room, and when we arrived I slid the occupancy sign from the green circle to the red "X."

"You first," I said, refusing to waste any more of his time with my pointless efforts. He handed me his Spectrum Guide, and I flipped past his best-fit option to read aloud page two, his choice. "Dream Weaver. Desires and fears you leave bereft. For every warp and every weft. Replace one's will, with 3/1 twill. You let and take, dreams that enforce; dreams that create."

"Pretty much memorized that." He crouched down and crossed the pinky and ring fingers, as well as pointer and middle, on both hands. "But I can't make it work."

With twisted fingers in front of his face, he touched his thumbs together, mimicking the image in his Spectrum Guide. The Dream Weaver text and image weren't much, but they were a hell of a lot more than my Blank Canvas. If this didn't work, Jacob could always go back to his first page, which was supposed to be a better fit anyway. With an all but empty Spectrum Guide, I didn't have that luxury.

"Take a deep breath."

Jacob took a few frustrated breaths, and I drifted back to the problem of mounting grey. My doubt went deeper than the utility of Renegayd's actions. I had to deal with Enyo. Nobody knew about the queen's sister, but Enyo had planted a seed that took root to enhance my awareness of certain occurrences—disappearances—like she'd said. They were easy to miss, because LGBT recruits filled the queen's Ivory Tower faster than it emptied.

"Did you know the girl with red hair who used to eat breakfast the same time as us sometimes?"

He laughed, as I leafed through the eight pages in his Spectrum Guide, ignoring his grunting attempts to will the power to control dreams.

"No," he answered. "And that is the most vague description of someone ever."

"Come on. The Scales have been like clockwork these past few weeks. This girl was always a few tables down from us."

"What about her? Got a crush?" he joked.

"Yes. Yes that's it Jacob. I wanted to tell you that I'm going back in the closet." I thought about what it could mean. "It's just weird. I mean she's there all the time, and then she's not."

"Maybe she got a girlfriend, or a new breakfast spot, or changed her alarm."

"Maybe… I've noticed a few others. It's funny how you can be close to someone and not realize it until they aren't there anymore."

"What's going on with you?" He leaned over to study the page in his Spectrum Guide. "Not trying to sound like a jerk, but maybe you should practice Blank Canvas-ing more than philosophizing about missed connections."

I pointed to the image of the cute guy twisting his fingers like Jacob mimicked. "This guy's got a tail. You think you'll look different when you get your power?"

"I don't care," he said. "That guy is hot, and this power is badass. If I'm meant to have a tail, than I can think of some fun things to do with it."

I shoved him away laughing, and he went back to practicing. "I'm not philosophizing. I guess what I'm saying is that it seems like something strange might be going on. Brun-Brun disappeared, and—"

"Sam, please." Jacob cut me off. "Can we please talk about something else? We're fighting for global LGBT equality and unlocking comic book powers."

"Keep your thumbs together," I redirected.

"Thank you," he said. "You want to try for a bit?"

"Maybe later," I said, and went back to reading his guide.

Jacob took another deep breath, but then broke form. "You know, you might be able to do some good for Renegayd if you tried."

"Excuse me?" My back straightened at the sucker punch.

"You're supposed to have an all powerful ability, and you want to talk about this Brun-Brun guy ditching you. He's gone. Get over it. If you spent half the time you spend moping trying to get even a fraction of the queen's power, you could shape the whole cause."

"The queen avoids all my questions! Don't you think that's a little strange?"

"Do you hear yourself? Don't you think she's a busy running Renegayd? Fighting for your rights? The queen welcomed you! She brought you into her Scales of Justice, and you're mad she won't cozy up for a chat about your boy problems. It's ridiculous!"

"I don't want to chat about boy problems." I couldn't help but defend myself. "I'm just not as ready as you are to buy into all her bullshit."

"Bullshit? Is that what you think of Perfect Equality?"

"Perfect Equality, right." I gave up.

I wanted to ask if he thought that's really all that was going on, but from his perspective, I *was* being ridiculous. He didn't have the same seed of doubt that made everything fit Enyo's warning. Jacob didn't know the half of it, and his reaction confirmed that I couldn't share more. He took his Spectrum Guide back.

"I'm sorry," he said. "Scales business is stressful, and I want to get my power. Why don't we practice separately today?"

"Fine. I'm sorry too."

I left thinking how sorry I was for our different reactions. It was our job to see grey, to give it a name and a value, and a fit into utility equations. But the more I saw, the more difficult everything became. I may have been a Blank Canvas, but Jacob was more like the queen than I'd ever be. The more they saw, the easier things became.

That's why I was sorry. I was jealous, with its layers and complexity and intensity pushing me further from my friend and from the Scales. The more distant I became, the closer I felt to Brun-Brun. With more context on the queen and her army, I understood that in the moment he'd provided his warning, and I'd rejected it, we'd both been right. That was the ultimate "Scales-thought." Both of us being correct—when they appeared mutually exclusive—was the type of twisted thought that held no value beyond endless debate and Freshmen philosophy class.

Who was right didn't matter. Those beliefs became actions and what mattered took shape. Random shit scrambled everything anyway, until neither the beliefs nor the actions were recognizable, and after all the somersaulting logic it came down to a simple truth with a depressing new lens: reality is the only thing that matters.

For now, reality meant months of making the best of an increasingly dangerous situation. Suspicion rose; Mission Morality's evil grew; Renegayd's extremism corresponded;

tension across the Scales stewed; the queen's resolve hardened; my fear intensified. And round and round reality went, increasing my desire to disconnect from it if the guilt from doing so wouldn't set the whole carousel back in motion.

Chapter 12

The News Cycle

Mission Morality was organized. In the ten months since Renegayd's coming out— and their first attacks—they set up a headquarters in the Rub' al Khali, a blistering part of the Arabian Desert. It wasn't that the Middle East had more hate to organize, but it did have more useless land. Hate organized itself, culminating in a literal fortress constructed in the desert. It was built in secret, but—just as people had flocked to the Mission Morality label—as soon as their HQ was revealed, thousands felt called to move to it.

"You know," Adele said, "Mission Morality's fortress is sort of like Gairyland. People like living in echo chambers."

"Sure," Benj laughed. "'Cept it's hot as blazes, sand blowin' everywhere, with no natural food or water."

"Amen to that, Baby." Shǎng kissed Benj. "Gays win again!"

We clinked glasses and sipped ecstasy. Pansy's Pub-erty was

crowded. It was rare that we were out of the tower while the rest of the city was still alive. Late nights, early mornings, and ragers between campaigns blurred days into months.

"Who knew saving the world would feel this great?" Jacob joked, spilling a bit of Orgie.

"Oh, is that what we're doing?" Lou said with a laugh.

"Yeah," Jacob defended. "Two countries have legalized homosexuality already; there's more support for Perfect Equality than Mission Morality; and when we started, getting in the news at all was a win."

"Legalizing homosexuality." Adele rolled her eyes. "How ridiculous."

"Not when the opposite is jail or death."

"I get it." Adele took a sip and her eyes rolled back this time. "I just mean, *what the fuck*? What kind of world do we live in?"

"That's why we live in this one!" Jacob said, pointing to the table holding our Orgies.

"That's still home," Adele said. "This is my vacation home."

"Hell of a vacation." Jacob almost fell out of his chair.

I snuck glances at the News Cycle map hung on the pub wall. The queen had provided every public place with a News Cycle map that acted like an update countdown clock. Pansy's Puberty hung theirs on the wall behind Benj. Transparent pegs marked landmarks on the simplified city map. One peg glowed orange, and then it shut off and the next peg lit up, moving from Transpo Hub Square up Main Street toward the Ivory Tower.

"Hell-lo!" Benj waved his hands over his head, breaking my view of the map. "Come on. We don't do this often. The news can wait."

"You're right." I took a sip of Orgie, which seemed to satisfy him. "Used to be my news was cat videos and gay Putin memes. Now, it's a report card."

"Yer putin' on too much pressure—" Benj waited for me to laugh, but map's light moved one notch closer to Pansy's. "Christ, come on. But after, you gotta promise you'll stay and drink too much. Only excuse for leavin' is goin' home with someone. You need it. Been tighter than a drag queen's balls."

He sat up as the map's orange light moved up Main Street, one peg away from Pansy's.

"Deal," I said and hurried for the door.

The News Cycle rolled up the street into view, and on queue, the sidewalk packed with people clambering for updates. They poured out of nearby bars and flats, either boredom or fascination fueling their consumption. Its addictiveness was inarguable. The queen knew how to manipulate her people—the Scales of Justice proved that—but the News Cycle was her latest. Just seeing it roll down the street made me salivate.

"It's so queen." Benj laughed, and then opened his mouth.

Missing could be messy; so, we stood on the curb with our mouths open. All conversation paused until the News Cycle rolled passed.

The operator was a Juggler. His Spectrum ability let him do more things at one time than was otherwise humanly possible. He operated the giant wheel that rolled up Main Street with his left pinky, while his other four fingers tapped different buttons, customized for his comfort. His right hand pulled levers behind him, spun dials above and below, and saluted the enthusiastic consumers crowding the street.

The News Cycle looked like a two-story, human hamster wheel. Three concentric circles surrounded the Juggler, who sat on a single pole in the innermost circle, pedaling like mad. His pedal-power spun the outermost ring, a tank tread propelling the News Cycle through the city twenty-four-seven. The machine was fueled by the Juggler's incredible multitasking and the Orgie that kept him going, obtained through a long straw inches from the Juggler's mouth. Immediate refreshment—plus benefits—whenever needed.

"On the hour every hour! Money, fame, sex, and power! Prim and proper. Gross and gory. Open up, receive your story!"

As the News Cycle passed, the middle ring distributed updates. It rotated in the opposite direction as the other two and fired streams of update juice into people's open mouths from twenty or so mounted juice pistols. One unsuspecting bystander was sprayed straight in the face. She screamed and wiped the update juice off her forehead, licking her fingers as soon as the shock wore off.

Someone in the crowd shouted a thank-you, but most were already reacting to the taste of their updates. Falling to their knees, laughing, or pursing their lips.

A jolt of adrenaline raced through me as cold, wet update juice entered my mouth. Designed to always be delicious no matter what it conveyed, I had to get past the taste to see the news. The queen had created a liquid so sophisticated it could tell stories, but it didn't require a sommelier's palate. This was brute-force communication, milliseconds gave the gist and a few quick swirls analyzed it. Beyond fresh ambrosial flavors, I received news of death—an attack—Mission Morality.

Benj grabbed my arm as he tasted the headlines.

"Go!" He said, pushing me back toward Pansy's. "Somethin' happened!" He shouted to everyone in the bar. "Mission Morality… they're killin' people!"

"Hold up, baby." Shǎng calmed Benj with his Empath ability.

"Sam and I caught the News Cycle. Mission Morality's killed thousands. Gay, straight, it doesn't matter anymore. They're exterminatin' us."

I hadn't swallowed my update juice to make sure it was fresh. Swishing it once more, I swallowed and relayed my update.

"They're calling us a disease. Saying they're removing the area surrounding the cancer to eliminate it. Allies, anybody in favor of Perfect Equality."

"How many?" Adele asked.

"It's still happening," I answered, losing the update's freshness already. "They hacked into the global equality poll's results, and are targeting anyone in support of equality. They've declared war on the whole LGBT community. More than thirty countries are reporting attacks."

"Fuck," Jacob said.

A downpour of glitter fell on the empty barstool next to Jacob. "Fuck indeed!" the queen agreed, crossing her legs. "It's horrible. Just horrible. *But*, every fuck brings new opportunity. This is our chance."

Chapter 13

Picking Sides

Do more. That's what the queen wanted.

The attack's indiscriminate nature and the resulting senseless loss of life showed how dangerous things were now—or had always been—for LGBT people. Closeted, out, proud, ashamed... dead. There was no plan yet to debate, and the queen sat back, watching the council chamber, while her Scales of Justice fumed.

"We need a list of our most powerful Spectrum abilities." Jacob's anger fueled energy. "We have to respond immediately."

Adele hadn't said a word since entering the Scales room.

Lou was scared. "What if we make it worse?"

"It will get worse," Jacob said. "Mission Morality preys on vulnerability. They feel stronger kicking us while we're down, and they'll keep going. It won't stop. We have to shut them down, or more people will die."

For the first time, I truly felt like a Blank Canvas. Not powerful: empty. I didn't know how to feel. It was hard to fathom what had happened, to have an appropriate reaction to overwhelming loss, but I didn't feel anger. I didn't feel fear, either, not on this side of the closet doors. We were safe, and there was guilt for that. But, overshadowing all of it, I felt responsibility. We'd escalated things.

"Calm down," I started. "We can't overreact."

"Overreact!" Jacob guffawed.

"I mean we can't be careless. Everything causes something else to happen."

"Sounds pretty careless to take our time while people die!" Jacob fired back. "They declared war. That's a pretty clear challenge."

"These aren't your middle school bullies, Jacob. We can't beat them up after PE class."

"Fuck you!"

"You two chill." Benj broke things up. "We need to figure out if we're doin' everything we can do."

"Oh, come on, Benj," Jacob said. "Haven't you been around the Spectrum long enough to know there's no such thing as *everything we can do*? There's nothing we can't do."

The queen paced by the window overlooking the clouds below.

"We knew things wouldn't change overnight," I said. "Mission Morality's practically been at war with us since day one. Declaring it doesn't change that. This hurts, but it helps our cause. Think of the sympathy they've built for equality by making its absence so painful."

"That's exactly what we set out to avoid!" the queen said, taking over the conversation. "Renegayd forces change! We don't wait for it."

"Renegayd's been cheap birthday magic so far," Jacob said. "We need to show real power. Let Mission Morality *know* we won't stand by while they kill the people we promised to liberate!"

"We're a movement for equality, not an army!" I said.

"They're not beating us in the polls! They're beating us in the streets!"

"Sweet Tarts," the queen interrupted, "I have a plan. Rainbow graffiti, media takeovers, global recruitment… the enemy's cornered. That's where hate is, cowering in corners, in alleyways and locker rooms. Spineless, waiting until love's outnumbered."

"What do you want to do?"

"Meet them there. Fight the individuals who hate. Get Renegayd on the ground and protect the people we set out to protect—look for hate and crush it. Provide security for every gay in the world. The ultimate bodyguard."

"There are millions of LGBT people," Lou said. "We can't protect them all."

"Then, we'll do whatever we can. Put Renegayd members around the world and livestream whenever we help. Real-life, real-time bully prevention."

"How do we find them?" Jacob asked. "We need Cerebro."

"Empaths," the queen said, forcing everyone's attention to our resident Empath.

"I could try to tune into fear," Shǎnguāng said.

"Or hate," Benj added.

"It's the same channel," said the queen. "Empaths identify where we can help. We share those locations to our people around the world. Attacks, bullying, injustice... we get our people there to help. With any luck, the idea of being confronted by a Renegayd will decrease harm."

We were scared, angry, ready to bless almost anything. The Scales of Justice had never gelled like this. There would be no debate if I didn't speak up.

"What if it does the opposite?" I said. "That's what happens with recruiting... with everything we do."

"This is different," Jacob said. "We tell people we're doing whatever it takes."

"Sounds reckless. Another escalation."

"Let's do it," the queen said. "If everyone's in agreement, I think we can give it a shot."

"We haven't even discussed it!" I urged. "The Scales of Justice is supposed to weigh every possibility—the pros and cons, assess the utility—and *then* decide! We've barely talked!"

Jacob popped out of his seat, approaching the chalkboard to write an equation using the variables we'd created to represent loss of life, emotional damage, time to equality, and other factors on both sides.

"They. Are. Killing. Us," he said as he scribbled. "This is clearly Utility Positive."

"It's a mistake," I said. "It's Utility Positive, because Mission Morality is causing runaway harm!"

"The cost of waiting is too high. There's no time, Sam." Jacob looked at the queen. "I'm in."

"Me too," Shǎng crushed my fleeting hope.

Lou joined them. "There's a lot to work out, but I think we can pull it off."

Benj nodded in agreement, and Adele was in too.

"Sam?" the queen asked. "What do you think?"

"We're putting our people in unnecessary danger. Scattering them around the world and then instigating violence."

Jacob replied, "Renegayd's put more innocent, uninvolved lives in danger than our own. That doesn't feel very just to me."

"Renegayd's a tool for good. We don't need to melt the whole hammer to remove a nail."

The queen cackled. "Baby, that's butch! Didn't think you knew nothin' about hammers."

"Mission Morality is going to fuck this up," I said. "People will get hurt."

"They'll try," said the queen. "But we can't sit in safety while they hate crime all over everything. Let's do it."

"We can't!" I protested. "It's not unanimous. I don't agree."

"Woman's prerogative, Honey. I changed my mind about that unanimous rule. Jacob, write up the decision. We'll distribute today."

"This isn't justice," I said. "It's a crime."

The queen's face lit up. "It's a *Love Crime*. That's what we'll call it."

The End of the Rainbow

Chapter 19

Resistance

Out of the shadow of the Ivory Tower, the queen's presence was stronger than ever. Like the sinking dread of sleep paralysis, I couldn't move or shout, but something heavy and just out of view threatened to crush me. Now though, it was a waking nightmare. I could scream, but for what? I could run, but from what? The weight of reality remained inescapable.

The queen gave me an army, but the queen's sister gave us somewhere to go. Enyo conveniently came out of hiding to offer sanctuary in her secret compound beneath the forest outside the city, moving my reunion with Brun-Brun out of the Ivory Tower's cavernous basement to a place we could rehash the first thing he'd said after the cages lifted.

"How did this happen?"

"Dionysia." I said, recounting the months—recruitment, Mission Morality, their war—but still struggling to answer what

I knew was at the heart of his question. "You warned me. I know"

"I did," he said.

"She was imprisoning people in secret, removing anyone who disagreed with her. I looked for you. I was suspicious. The Scales—" I stumbled trying to explain what had happened since we'd last seen each other. "We tried to control it, to make Renegayd something good. But I thought— we all thought—. We were doing real good!"

"Nothing you described sounds like good."

"But maybe it will be worth it," I thought back to our equations.

"People are dead! *I* was lock— your frien—." His anger made the downgrading of our relationship apparent. "She's wrecking havoc on both sides of the closet doors!"

"It wasn't that clear. It wasn't so black-and-white."

He nodded, and in that motion disconnected. I wanted to embrace him; to satiate longing that had grown from months of searching. Lust maybe, but our perspectives weren't as far apart as he thought.

"I agree with you. That's why I left. I don't think the queen is right."

"Hmm," he said, growing the distance between us by disregarding it, and that's how it stayed.

Enyo tended to the wounds of my freed captives. She was curious why the queen would create an army, hand me the reins, and then disappear, but the opportunity distracted her from seeing what I did: that this was a trap. The queen knew where we were—probably wanted us here—holed up underground, Enyo trying to control the queen's puppet, pretending the strings weren't still attached.

"Sam, your support will raise our chances." Enyo didn't hide her desire for anyone but me to be sitting across from her glower in her compound. "The resistance will continue with or without you, of course, but these people trust you. We want their hearts in it. Need to fire them up. Remind them this is their chance to fight back." She handed me a piece of paper. "You need to read this tomorrow."

Brun-Brun avoided eye contact by staring at the table with his arms crossed, and I attempted to lure a reaction.

"What do you think, Brun-Brun?" I tried.

Enyo sighed, and Brun-Brun ignored me. This had become tradition. One bird spread its feathers and danced around, while the other pretended not to notice, and a third shit all over everything.

Repeating what she'd said daily for two weeks, Enyo hoped to beat me into submission. "We must act fast. You need to let me know if you're with us or not."

"You're sure this is the only way?" I asked.

"Of course I'm not sure." Enyo's disgust at the question, at the inconvenience of our forced alliance, subjugated her words. "It's the best we've got. It's a chance."

"It could go wrong. I'm not sure."

"There's still some tricks up my sleeve." Enyo smiled at the little girl at the end of the table.

It was the same girl she'd been with when Adele and I ran into her at the Transpo Hub. At most half my age, Imprint sat quietly apart from the adults, so it was easy to forget she was there at all. She watched, bored, kicking her feet back and forth.

"I don't want anyone to get hurt," I said.

That got a reaction. Popping out of his chair, Brun-Brun reached across the table to scold me.

"People already got hurt! *You* hurt them! This is your chance to do the right thing. For once!"

"Hey!" Adele shouted.

"Don't get me started." Brun-Brun pointed at her. "You're all guilty."

He stormed out, leaving Enyo waiting for my answer.

"Fine! I'll say whatever you want," I conceded before hurrying after Brun-Brun.

He was gone by the time I got to the hallway, and I regretted following after. A girl gasped, then cheered, when she saw me. The underground compound was filled with freed prisoners. I was a celebrity living with my biggest fans. They assumed what the queen said was true: that everything I did was part of some great plot to ruin her, that I really had saved them. Of course they assumed that. Why would she make it up? I sure as hell didn't understand it.

Two boys snickered when they saw me.

"What?!" I shouted.

"—a lovely day!" Adele corrected, threading her arm through mine to pull me through the hall. "What was that about?"

"Christ! You don't want me to read that for Enyo?" I said.

"Simmer. I'm talking about Brun-Brun. What's his deal? We were trying to help. Things got out of control, and we left… saving his ass in the process."

"He told me this would happen. From the minute I got here, he was trying to get me to help him and Enyo, and I didn't listen."

"Lot of good he did trapped in that pit." Adele changed her tone. "We need to find the others. If you're going along with this, we need a plan."

*****

"Comrades."

The word sounded awkward. The whole speech did, piped from the wired microphone to the whole compound. Enyo's prepared statement was all lies, adding to the paltry scene.

"This is Sam DeSalvo, with Benj, Shǎnguāng, and Adele, the defectors from the queen's Scales of Justice. Before we make our first move of resistance against the queen, we wanted to remind you that there is no justice in anything Renegayd does. For the queen, justice has nothing to do with this war. Believe me. I've seen her plans from the inside."

As I read the first lie, I looked at Enyo standing next to her secret weapon, a little girl giving more attention to a freckle on her arm than the mission.

"The queen plans…" I was supposed to tell everyone the queen was planning on destroying the world. That was Enyo's calculation for what would instill enthusiasm to resist. "What the queen's planning…. Look." I went off script. "The truth is, I don't know what the queen is planning."

Enyo lurched from the corner toward the table, stopping short of yanking the microphone off the table.

"What I do know is that she's already incited more violence than is just. I joined Renegayd because I believed in what she was doing. I believed equality was worth any cost. Sitting on the Scales of Justice meant seeing that cost every day, arguing about it, and deciding, even as things got worse, that equality outweighed the harm it took to achieve."

Enyo struggled against Brun-Brun, who kept her from interjecting.

"The queen doesn't care," I continued. "The harm Renegayd causes doesn't matter to her. She's imprisoned her own followers, killed thousands, endangered more. This will get worse, but the queen doesn't care. Apathy is why I left. For her, the end justifies any means. It was never that end I rejected. I rejected her path. I do care how we obtain equality. The queen doesn't."

I leaned back, and Brun-Brun let Enyo loose to rip the microphone chord from the wall.

"What the hell are you doing?" She turned to Brun-Brun. "And what was that? We need them to hate the queen! How do you expect people to fight apathy?"

Adele answered, "Nobody's fighting anything, remember?"

She looked around the room, outnumbered. "Fine! We're getting out of here." Enyo grabbed Imprint's hand.

"One more thing," Benj interjected.

"What?" Enyo hissed.

"We're comin' with you."

"Absolutely not."

"We're not celebrity tributes," Benj said. "We know the plan. So we join you, or run to the front lines and tell everybody what yer really up to."

"Don't even need to run there," Shǎng said, pointing to his temple. "I can let them know right now."

Enyo's face twisted. I couldn't read Brun-Brun's reaction, but he stayed quiet.

"This is our one shot," she said. "Stay out of my way. If we mess this up, it's over."

Enyo spun around clutching the little girl's hand. I turned to Brun-Brun wanting to explain that this meant the Scales were finished putting others in harm's way while we sat on the sidelines, but he rushed past me, taking his place beside Enyo.

Chapter 20

The Third Way

The seven of us climbed the stairs out of the compound. Blotches of sunlight leaked through a dense forest, bright and warm. People cheered when we waved. It felt right to be joining the charge.

"Group up! Group up!"

Enyo's original followers numbered in the tens, but they coordinated the whole army above ground.

"Group one!"

"Twos twos twos!"

Enyo had cataloged abilities the moment the freed prisoners set foot in her compound. I didn't like how these people, who'd suffered beneath the Ivory Tower, were bucketed into her labels, but the reasoning became clear. Our army was split into fourteen groups, each with one defensive Spectrum ability. The defectors from the Scales of Justice, Enyo, Brun-Brun, and the little-girl-secret-weapon made up the fifteenth group.

One by one, the groups jogged away from the compound, toward the city, protected by some Spectrum ability. Group three surrounded itself with a gelatinous lilac bubble. Another disappeared, rustling leaves the ability's sole tell.

"We're more than I'd planned," Enyo cursed. "There's a chance Renegayd reads us. So stay back."

Everything hinged on the fact that the one group who knew our real objective wouldn't be on the front lines. The queen's telepaths would read our front lines, and misinformation would flow back to her and—with any luck—buy us enough time.

I still didn't know Enyo's ability, but my friends would be sufficient protection. My contribution continued to be zero. Brun-Brun stayed next to Enyo, and once the second to last group had a solid head start, we followed behind. Beneath the forest's thick tangle of branches, the smell of trampled soil joined the morning dew that tickled my ankles as we jogged the trail blazed by our army to the forest's edge.

"Benj, take Imprint," Enyo instructed. "Straight for the Transpo Hub. No matter what."

Benj took two longer strides and swooped up the little girl, placing her on one shoulder. Between the forest and city, an open field stretched half a mile wide. If Renegayd didn't already know we were coming, it would be obvious when we charged into the field. My first steps into the open field were hot, exposed, and blind until my eyes adjusted to the sunlight. The Ivory Tower came into view, shooting into the sky, forever casting its shadow over the city.

"Shit!" Enyo directed my attention back to the field. "Brun-Brun!"

"I got it!" Adele tossed a fireball at a creature, which fell out of view into the tall grass before I got a look at it.

"What was that?" I asked.

No one responded, but Adele ignited her arms. Benj tossed the little girl into the air, shape-shifted, and caught her on his back to gallop on all fours across the field. Brun-Brun broke from the group in a zigzag path and jumped. With a graceful corkscrew, his wings unfurled, letting him take watch above.

"Woohoo!" I cheered, pumping my fist in the air.

"It's not a game," came Shǎng's recognizable voice within my mind. "Look there."

I felt him guide me to see what was happening. All fourteen groups were under attack. Disembodied tentacles slapped down at one, as if a massive squid swam beneath the field. A thick, pink cloud consumed another. One was chased by the ground itself, a rolling mound threatening to swallow them up if they fell.

Columns materialized at the edge of the city, one by one walling off the city with bars to keep us out.

"It's Dildee!" Shǎnguāng announced, and I recognized the pale blue statues.

"Can you reach 'em?" Benj shouted as we ran.

Shǎng left my mind, reaching out to explain to Dildee what we were doing: that the queen had imprisoned her own followers. We weren't his enemy.

"Shǎng?" Benj said as the statues' girth widened.

"Dildee says hi!" Shǎng answered.

The statues descended back into the ground the timer run out in our game of whack-a-cock. With the city accessible, its buildings seemed like refuge compared to the field's exposure.

Halfway there, Brun-Brun's shadow contorted. Adele screamed, and a quarter-sized rock smacked my forehead.

"Brun-Brun!"

The colorful rocks rained from above. Brun-Brun staggered in the air, flapping one wing while covering his body with the other, then clumsily switching back and forth to block the assault while remaining airborne. Whatever hit him fell on us, while more sailed into the forest.

"Got to be *Gobstopper!*" Adele yelled.

"I'll reach out to him!" Shǎng announced.

"GO UP!" I screamed, recognizing the colorful candy-bullets as another bizarre Spectrum ability. Brun-Brun ascended, and the barrage turned to us. Benj backpedaled to put his formidable werewolf body between Shǎng and I, cradling Imprint at his chest.

"He won't stop!" Shǎng said.

Each hit threatened to shatter whatever bone it struck, and Adele unfurled an umbrella of fire in front of us, melting the candies but blinding our progress.

"Almost there!" Shǎng said. "Don't let up. They're still coming. I can use Brun-Brun to see where we're going."

We tried running, but it was slower clumped behind Adele. I counted—one, two, three, four, five, six… someone was missing.

"Imprint!" I panicked. "She's gone!"

"She's doing her job!" Enyo panted. "Why. Do you think. We're running there?" She wasn't used to walking from place to place, let alone sprinting. "Get to the Transpo Hub!"

"Shǎng, did she do it?" I asked.

"Not yet."

That girl needed to rescue the others, or it wouldn't matter if we made it to Transpo Hub Square.

The field's soft ground collided with the stone streets of the city. Adele extinguished her fire. Gobstopper had either shifted his attack to some other group or repositioned for a better angle, and we weren't stopping to find out. It wasn't much further to Transpo Hub Square.

"Look out!"

Brun-Brun's warning drew our gaze up in time to see a tentacle plummeting—through a building—toward us. Brun-Brun slammed his shoulder into it, barely nudging the fleshy appendage as it snapped a street lamp. The ground shook, stones cracking in front of us under the weight of the tentacle.

"Go!" Benj hurdled the tentacle, and I scrambled onto and over it, as it lifted back up off the ground. The others ran beneath as another smashed the ground behind us.

"There's more!"

"Shit!"

Adele shot a blaze of fire down the street as a third tentacle flopped its way down the street. The monster fell through her flames, but with our retreat blocked by two more, Adele charged forward. The tentacle withered before finishing its descent, and whatever creature lay beneath retracted its appendages into craters that sealed back up behind them.

"What kind of fucked-up Spectrum ability is that?"

"Come on." Enyo took lead through familiar alleyways until we were finally adjacent to Transpo Hub Square. Peeking around one building, she extended her arm, stopping our advance.

She placed her finger over her lips, and Shǎng piped Brun-

Brun's vision into our own. Beneath the closet door statue, a Renegayd horde blocked the entrance to the Transpo Hub. One of our subgroups was already here—except they weren't supposed to be here at all. They were supposed to distract Renegayd by being anywhere but here.

From Brun-Brun's silent aerial perspective, we watched as the throng of Renegayd soldiers corralled our allies, forcing them toward the hub. The queen must have known where we were headed.

A tiny girl scurried out from beneath a store's sidewalk sign, underneath a giant's stilt-like legs, and into the center of our surrounded subgroup. The moment she reached them, they all disappeared. Renegayd pounced on the spot where our group had been, but there was nothing there: our secret weapon was doing her job. She was returning them all back to Enyo's compound.

"That's my girl! Nice work, Imprint," Enyo whispered. "Not full teleportation. She retraces her steps, back to anywhere she's been in the past two hours."

Spoiled by months of fighting people who were powerless against Spectrum abilities, Renegayd was confused. There was nothing to chase. So, the soldiers dispersed back into the streets. We stayed hidden until Brun-Brun gave the all-clear. Then, we ran for the Transpo Hub. Enyo wasted no time finding the London portal, a bumblebee-yellow closet door, amid hundreds of choices.

"Let's go," she said, throwing the door open.

"Home sweet home," replied Shǎng.

Brun-Brun landed beside me.

"Thank you," I said, and hurryied through the open door after Enyo.

Chapter 21

Transister

Through London's closet door, the Transpo Hub transformed into Enyo's back. Someone pushed me from behind, and we all toppled forward like dominos into a dark room.

"Oof."

"Get off me."

"What?"

"Ouch, fuck!"

Flailing, I caught hold of something that gave way under my weight. Dim light leaked into the one-hole bathroom as its door swung open, and we spilled out. A handsome man in a blazer waited for the commotion to end, before finding a spot to place his foot between our tangled bodies to continue over us for the restroom. He didn't seem bothered by the thought of a gangbang in the bathroom or by our presence at all.

Enyo picked herself off the floor and shushed us, disgusted.

"Oh, lay off, Enyo," Shǎng said. "Nobody gives two shits what we're doing so long as I'm here."

"Where are we?" I asked.

"Just go!" Enyo was embarrassed, despite the fact no one had so much as looked at us since we crashed through the door. "As if we haven't made a big enough scene. Jesus."

It was a bar—one I might have enjoyed under different circumstances. An old black-and-white movie played on the wall over a couple enjoying their happy hour cocktails. The décor almost seemed more fitting for the other side of the portal: fishbowls filled with goldfish, twinkling tile floors, and Barbies nailed to the ceiling.

Enyo led us past the bartender and out of the basement bar. We emerged into a random London alleyway beneath a sign on the brick wall reading *Friendly Society*.

"Heh! Old Compton! I got my first kiss there!" Shǎng pointed down the street at a big pink sign. "Let's stop in for a quick pint. For old times' sake!"

Enyo spun around. "Renegayd instigated the most violent day in LGBT history, we almost died not five minutes ago, and you want to grab a drink… for old times' sake?"

Shǎng made a pouty face. "Kinda."

"We're not far."

"You know I can turn everyone's calm on and off, right?"

Enyo ignored him and led us down the rainbow flag–lined street, past the Admiral Duncan, until we stopped in front of a long line of twinks waiting to get into G-A-Y.

"Oh sure… we can get a beer when *you* want one?" Shǎnguāng grumbled.

"The president of the Global Rights Organization agreed to meet us here." Enyo approached the purple double doors as a bouncer filled the entire space. "Excuse me."

"Card, please?" he demanded.

Enyo looked back at Shăng, who had let this one slip through his calming effect.

"Oh, yes, of course." Enyo showed her ID, and the bouncer smile.

"Not that, sweetheart. I believe you're over eighteen."

Shăng pranced forward, bumped Enyo out of the way, and held something at arm's length up toward the bouncer's face.

"Heeey," he said with his head cocked to one side. "How is it tonight?"

The muscle wall lumbered aside, jerked his thumb at the bar, and said, "You tell me."

"What is that?" Enyo asked with a heavy pinch of resentment.

"Gotta get that GAY card, bitches. Gets you into Heaven on Saturdays." He displayed a purple card with the white letters *G-A-Y*. "They're with me. Visiting from across the… pond. Can you pretty please—."

The bouncer, unimpressed, let us through.

"I'm gonna grab a beer. Have a fun meeting!" Shăng danced his way into the crowd, with Benj following after.

Enyo looked at the rest of us.

"Splitting up is a good idea," she admitted. "My brother might come looking for us. Apollo said he'd be on the third floor. Brun-Brun, come with me. Adele, you and Sam keep watch."

"Sam should come along." It surprised me to hear Brun-Brun suggest I do anything, and Enyo was too rushed to object.

"Come on," she snapped.

Brun-Brun nodded, and we made our way across the onyx dance floor, past the bar, to the corner staircase. Up the stairs, we traded first floor video screens playing the "Bad Romance" music video for ones showing "Let's Have a Kiki." It was impossible to guess the theme change—2000's to 2010's; Divas to Glam Rock; Gay Icons to Gay Groups? I would have preferred joining Adele, Shǎng, and Benj to find out, but I tried not to look too longingly at the party. Brun-Brun wanted me to join. He and Enyo believed an alliance with the Global Rights Organization could undo the queen's escalation. So, instead of joining the London gays, we climbed to the top floor.

The downstairs bass seeped up the stairs, into the top floor VIP lounge where a different song drowned out the Scissor Sisters. The thirty or so VIPs enjoyed more distinguished drinks in cocktail glasses and tumblers instead of bottles and cups like the other floors. Small, private groups kept to themselves, compared to the free-for-all beneath us. No one paid attention to us, except for a gentle-looking Hispanic man who walked straight up to Enyo, extending his hand.

"Apollo Vazquez," he said.

I couldn't help but look at Apollo's other hand, the one the queen had transformed on live TV. He caught me staring and held it up for closer examination. Sure enough, dangling right where his middle and ring fingers should have been was a ball sack.

"I keep it manscaped," he said. I didn't know how to react. Then Brun-Brun laughed, causing me to burst out with one loud guffaw.

"Well, you have a sense of humor about it." Enyo sounded disgusted.

"She did save my life," he said. "It's a reminder of what we're dealing with. That is— I can't pretend to know what we're dealing with."

"Our abilities make you uncomfortable, of course."

Enyo's volume seemed foolish compared to Apollo's. There was something about him that made me desperate to hear what he said, and embarrassed I couldn't hear his soft voice over the pounding bass—like this man didn't need to speak up, I needed to listen closer.

"Drink? Or shall we get to it?" he asked.

"We're fine," Enyo answered. "Thank you for meeting with us. We're big fans of your organization. I believe we can help each other."

"Yes," he said. "But let's sit first."

He led us from the corner staircase, across the rectangular room past the long bar. The video played some sort of artistic pornography instead of music videos. Naked men and women did what they do in gay porn but with heavy filmmaker influence: more or less shadows; prismatic or grayscale; intense close-ups or extreme distance. As we headed for a velvet purple couch opposite the stairs, a jiggling elbow changed into either a kneecap or a chin. If anything, whatever sexual act was happening seemed to match the rhythm of the VIP techno beat.

The other VIP's evaded our gaze. Even the bartender avoided eye contact, and I wondered if the whole bar was part of the Global Rights Organization. I couldn't believe its leader would meet us alone.

Apollo sat on one couch; Brun-Brun, Enyo, and I took the very edge of the other, trying to get close enough to hear him over the music. It was hard to avoid staring at the kaleidoscopic nipple on the screen above him.

Enyo seemed to realize the same thing I did. "This is not going to work," she said. "Do you mind if I quiet things down a bit?"

Apollo's face scrunched, but then he nodded.

A fluid membrane encircled us, obscuring everything. Lights became brighter in our area, while outside the music dulled. The membrane liquefied the art-porn—its image melting into watercolor raindrops that dripped down the sides of the bubble—and the distance between our corner and the others in the VIP lounge seemed to stretch.

"Ah. There!" Enyo smiled.

At the edge of his seat, Apollo squinted to see the now-amorphous shapes that were the other VIPs.

"Don't worry," Enyo reassured. "We haven't moved. They're still there. Ready to pounce on us if needed."

Enyo smiled, and Apollo blushed. He became more animated. "That *is* a trick!"

"Mine is quite mundane," she said.

"Spectrum abilities…" Apollo took a deep breath. "What do you call this one?"

"*Attentive.* We hear things, but we rarely listen. Attentive helps us hear each other. Body language, vocal tones, eye twitches—there's so much to communication. This makes things easy. Of course, I can stop anytime."

It was clear in the way she said it that Enyo did not want to stop using her ability, but that she was willing. Perhaps that clear intent demonstrated the Attentive effect.

"I'm fine with it," Apollo said. And I understood he was indeed fine with it, but also uncomfortable with the idea the she could influence the conversation.

Enyo adjusted farther back on the couch, tossed her hair, and tried to get more comfortable—clearly preparing for the meat of the conversation.

Apollo started. "Love Crimes was a tragedy."

"I agree."

"And these abilities in the news, in this bar, have everything to do with it."

"I understand. Had it been my choice, I would not have revealed the existence of the other world."

Apollo rubbed his temple with his ball-free hand. "Yes, the other world. It's all overwhelming, to be honest. The fact there is something like that to reveal at all. Abilities like this ask for inflated retaliation. It isn't only Mission Morality, it's world governments, everyday people."

"Things are going to get worse," Enyo said. "The leader of Renegayd, the one called 'the queen,'" her lip flared when she said it, "Believes all this is peeling back the façade. Showing the depth of hate that must be overcome before Perfect Equality can be achieved."

"What is this Perfect Equality she keeps describing? People don't appease demands down the barrel of a gun. It wouldn't matter if she was promoting drinking water; you appear out of nowhere with magic spells, matching outfits, and propaganda, and people will lose it." Enyo nodded. "Which is the very thing you've done."

That stopped her nodding. *You* meant all of us. Enyo, Brun-Brun, me... not just the queen.

"Yes," she said. It was hard to disagree. We weren't Renegayd, but our army fit his description. "That is what I wanted to talk to you about—an alliance, a collaboration between worlds. If you succeed in disrupting Renegayd's plans, you will become a target. Once that happens, you know you can't win. We can protect you from Renegayd and from Mission Morality. You're making enemies, and we can be powerful friends."

"Why? If you're so powerful, why ally with the Global Rights Organization?"

"You share this world with Mission Morality, and we share ours with Renegayd. Both enemies of the change we're seeking, and neither can be beaten alone."

Enyo's Attentive bubble brought clarity to the whole conversation: Enyo's vulnerability and fear of her sister; Apollo's skepticism and confusion.

The leader of the Global Rights Organization rested his head in his hand, the scrotum dangling beneath his chin. "A few months ago, I was running the London chapter of an AIDS awareness organization. Now, I'm running a global movement caught between a group that is killing us out of hate and another that could do so by snapping. I don't want this responsibility."

Enyo looked at me. This was my time. "I felt the same way. I'm from San Francisco. Someone tricked me into crossing over. Since then, I've been running away from all of this." I looked at Brun-Brun. "This partnership is the right thing to do. Give yourself a little credit. We reached out to you. We want to help you."

"I knew you wanted an alliance," he said, "but let's be honest—not like your listening bubble-thing would allow anything else—we can't possibly work together. You scare people. You scare me."

"We want the same thing. Peaceful resistance, non-violent change!" Enyo sounded desperate, a side effect of her Attentive bubble. "Why bother meeting if it were truly impossible?"

"I was curious," Apollo answered. "It's so unbelievable, I thought that maybe seeing people like you would help me understand it, but an alliance...." He laughed. "Look, there's no way the Global Rights Organization can *officially* partner."

The word "officially" slipped its way into Apollo's comment, surprising even him.

"Ah," Enyo said. "I hope you don't mind how evident what you're proposing is. So, you do see how we can help each other." He was embarrassed. "Something unofficial."

"Of course having these powers on our side could help, but you must see how our meeting puts the movement at risk. The Global Rights Organization has stood against everything your world has done. I don't trust you, but even this bubble has countless ways it could help."

"Sounds like we'll be used," Enyo said.

"You wanted a partnership. We're going to have to start slow. At this point, there isn't much for the Global Rights Organization to gain."

No hint of confusion. Apollo wanted an unofficial partnership or nothing at all.

"There is a lot to gain," Enyo said. "You haven't even been to the other side. We can take you there. Show you what you're up against."

Apollo seemed appalled by the suggestion. "You can't recruit me."

"We don't want to recruit you," I tried. "We want to work together."

"Don't you see that by partnering we'll be hurting our own image? You must see that."

"Yes, but—" the length of my pause before completing the sentence made my agreement apparent.

Enyo gave me the death stare, and inside the bubble it meant... a death stare. I tried to avoid it, but her gaze burned through me. Nobody said anything. Even the muffled beat of the techno soundtrack ceased. Enyo wasn't staring at me; she was frozen. Mid-negotiation—Apollo, Enyo, Brun-Brun, even the distant shadows outside our bubble—nobody moved. Nobody except a tall mirage that grew as it approached the bubble. The *tap-tap-tap* of stilettos became more pronounced when it crossed the membrane.

"Oh Baby, shut that mouth 'fore you drool all over the velvet couch," said the Queen of Witches. "I know it's this dress that's got your tongue. Fabulous, right?" She spun, and her long, beaded dress took on the colors of G-A-Y.

"What are you doing here?" I asked. Enyo's bubble showcased my fear.

"Honey Cakes, what are *you* doing here?" She pointed a clip-on fingernail at me. "This is some sad, desperate shit. Ivory Tower to London pub. Ooh, how the mighty have fallen."

"If you're going to kill me, get on with it."

"Kill you?" The queen cackled. "How many times do you have to say that before you understand? I've invested way too much in you. You remember what it was like up in the Ivory Tower, running the Scales of Justice? Balancing all those equations. You loved it. I was clearing the way for your work." I opened my mouth to reply, but she kept on talking. "All the rest of it—the decisions and the plotting and the leadership you gave to Renegayd—that was all you. I'd rather thank you than kill you."

It was hard to ignore her prodding, the constant pushing that begged for a reaction.

"I'm through with you," I said.

"Fine." Her expression grew wide and wild. She flicked her hand, and an invisible force threw me out of my seat, pinning me against the wall. The queen turned her attention to the velvet couch and positioned herself in front of her sister.

With a snap of the queen's finger, Enyo choked back into motion, gasping for air. When she saw the queen standing across from her, she fell over trying to run.

"Ha!" the queen barked. "Nice to see you too! What a warm welcome."

Enyo didn't hesitate. She reached over and tapped Brun-Brun on the head. He jolted back to life with a gasp.

"Brun-Brun!" I shouted. "The queen!"

He took a strong stance between Enyo and the queen. His soft white glow reminded me how he'd saved me. I hoped he'd do so again.

"Oh heey, B," the queen said casually.

"Get her!" Enyo shouted from behind him, and Brun-Brun charged.

"No!" I screamed, but the queen was quick.

She unsheathed her wand and shook it like a three-year old shaking her birthday present. Brun-Brun glided over to the wall next to me, struggling to break the bond I'd given into.

"Still encouraging others to do your dirty work." The queen backed Enyo into the corner between the two couches, inches from where Apollo remained frozen in place.

"If it's a battle of power," Enyo said, "you know I can't match you. Never could."

"Oh, I don't know. You seem quite comfortable showing your power over me. Remember?"

"Of course I remember. Though, I never dreamed you'd take things this far, Dennis."

The queen's eyes flared when her sister used that name. "Don't call me that. And don't you dare claim responsibility for Renegayd."

"I wish I didn't feel responsible. Honest. I couldn't lie in here even if I wanted to, which I don't." Enyo gestured to the bubble she'd formed. "I'd take back everything if I thought it would do any good."

The queen feigned amusement. "This is real nice. Two sisters talking real with each other. Sharing our feelings. You know? I think we can work this out."

Enyo dropped the apologetic tone. "You're either daft or thick. Don't you realize you're letting our history destroy this world?"

"You can't even let me have Renegayd. It has to be what *you* did that fuels this whole thing."

"Then there'd be at least some twisted reason behind all this, some chance to end it! You followed me all the way here. So what? I'm sorry! Is that what you want? Here—in the Attentive bubble—I'm sorry!"

Maybe that was all it would take, an apology for some childhood feud that sparked everything.

The queen looked at Enyo without responding. Just looked at her. Beneath their masks—one of glitter, the other of fear—the siblings looked similar. Then the glitter turned to stone. Lips squeezed, wand ready, the queen responded.

"Try as I might, you'll always be more of a cunt than I could ever be. Only a twisted bitch would think that miserable apology would make things okay."

The queen made the first deliberate wand flick I'd seen.

Blood sprayed from her sister's throat, a carbonated bottle's explosive pressure released before red liquid spluttered down its side, and the bottle fell.

"Oh God!" I still couldn't move.

Enyo's scream was short. The Attentive bubble dissipated when she hit the ground. There was so much blood. Brun-Brun was shouting, still stuck to the wall next to me. He looked sad, but it was hard to tell if he looked at the body on the floor or the one standing over it.

The queen's chin quivered. Her wand lowered, and I came unstuck, though I still didn't dare to approach the queen. I started to say something, to verbalize what had happened, but the queen turned. Her face was hard, victorious, and I couldn't find the words. Maybe her chin hadn't quivered.

"Don't. You. Dare," she said, turning to Brun-Brun.

He deflated, the queen's gaze diverting his to the floor. She stood with her back to the frozen VIP lounge looking with pursed lips at the result of our Global Rights Organization meeting.

"Think you got your ally," she said, nodding to Apollo. "Sam, you are the Blank Canvas, she was never meant to control what you have. Renegayd is finishing this. We're taking the fight to their doorstep. One week. Then we destroy Mission Morality's fortress along with their hatred."

"Please," I said. "Isn't this enough? Attacking will make things worse. You can't extinguish hate."

"You're wrong," she said. "We're the only ones who can."

Brun-Brun took a deep breath.

The queen smiled. "Gawd, you two. Quite the power couple."

And she was gone, her glitter pool left to float in Enyo's blood. The rush of music was accompanied by in-sync gasping for air as the room's occupants jerked back to life. All but one. Apollo screamed, jumping away from Enyo's collapsed body at his feet. Brun-Brun hurried to position himself between her body and the rest of the room.

"Get Shǎng!" he shouted, while trying to calm Apollo.

By the time I reached the staircase, the VIP lounge had noticed. A piercing scream and flurry of moving bodies disappeared as I descended to the first floor, scrambling to find the others. Shǎng dropped his drink when I told him what happened, screamed when he saw the body, and wailed even as he stood in the opposite corner of the VIP floor, using Empath to return things to relative calm.

Apollo's shock let Brun-Brun attempt an explanation—the queen's attack, Enyo's familial ties, the warning about Renegayd's next campaign. It had been the blink of an eye for Apollo.

"We don't stand a chance, do we?" Apollo said.

"I don't know," said Brun-Brun. "But Renegayd attacking Mission Morality's fortress, is going to make things worse."

Apollo thought out loud. "How can she do this? What possible moral compass makes her think this is just?"

Brun-Brun looked at me.

"Utilitarianism—or some bastard version," I explained. "The positive or negative of each Renegayd action is weighed. Variables for possibilities, all plugged into an equation to make sure the result is Utility Positive."

"What conceivable positive is coming from this?" he asked.

"Think of all the pain and suffering of being gay," I explained. "If you're lucky, there's just hiding, and bullying, and early years of being closeted. If not, there's more extreme abuse: emotional and physical… lives lost to suicide and murder."

Apollo pondered that—thanks to Shǎng's calming presence—and responded, "Nothing is as frightening as flawed moral logic. Sounds like you're missing the most important variable in your equation."

"What?"

"Mission Morality wants to kill Renegayd, and Renegayd wants to kill Mission Morality. But the real enemy is hate. We should be attacking that."

"Agreed," said Brun-Brun. "I think I know how."

They had found some common ground I missed.

"What? What are you talking about?" I said.

"You wanted an ally, right?" Apollo patted my shoulder.

I looked at Brun-Brun, at Enyo's body, and then nodded. The queen was right—she'd pushed things along, no doubt confident in whatever trade-offs she saw in helping us. We had our ally and a plan, and the queen had her revenge.

A little bit of my soul died in G-A-Y as I contemplated how Enyo, facedown in a pool of her own blood, might have helped us stop the cycle of hate by solidifying an alliance. So close to the ramification of the equation, I still imagined each variable on the chalkboard. Utility Positive.

Chapter 22

Progress

"She's alive." That fact shocked everyone except Brun-Brun, who brought the news to the waiting room.

"How the heck she manage that?" Benj said.

"The queen could have killed her," Brun-Brun said. "This must be what Dionysia wanted. For us to go on… without her sister."

"Given Enyo's queen-magnetism, that's not so bad," Shǎng grumbled.

"Why not kill her?" I asked.

"I don't know the whole story," Brun-Brun replied. "Only that Enyo never accepted her sister. Ironic, given she lived in the city built by Dionysia on that single principle. Enyo felt guilty about whatever happened between them, but she refused to accept her sister's transition. And, Dionysia obviously hasn't forgiven her."

"What if this was her final revenge?" I said. "Maybe it's behind them now."

"This won't end it," said Brun-Brun.

"Not the war, but whatever's going on between them. That may have made the queen who she is, but I believe her when she says this war is bigger than that. It has to be."

"And what about us?" he asked.

I'd rehearsed apologies and explanations and feelings, but in the London Welbeck Hospital waiting room, none of them seemed adequate.

"I should have listened. It all got... fucked up."

"Yeah," he said.

We sat in silence, masquerading as normal people in the normal world. An old woman shared the waiting room with us, a magazine open in her lap, hands wringing above it. I imagined her waiting for news of her husband, a lifetime together somehow bringing them here. Even a year spent exclusively surrounded by gays couldn't change the fact that in my mind, this woman was waiting for her husband.

I didn't notice Apollo until he spoke. "How is she?"

"Critical," Brun-Brun answered.

"I'm sorry." He let it settle, saying more with quiet than I could say with words. "I wish I could stay—."

"No, of course. We have a lot to prepare." Brun-Brun seemed to be pumping himself up.

"It's a good plan," Apollo said.

His confidence dredged a sinking in my stomach. The plan roused a familiar, dangerous feeling: certainty. I'd felt certain working on the Scales of Justice—not in our decisions, but in the process—and had been proven wrong.

"Apollo," I said, "before you go, can I ask you a question? It *feels* like we're doing the right thing, but how do we know it won't go wrong? What if we're wrong?"

"It's difficult." He didn't try to make it better. No deeper explanation to make the fear disappear.

"You're willing to risk your life on the guess that this will be more right than Renegayd or Mission Morality?"

He nodded. "That very act proves we're all human."

Shit. When did everyone become Confucius? Wisdom wasn't going to end this. I missed making decisions without analyzing their utility. I slid my hand down my face and let it go.

"Fine. Yeah. I guess that makes sense."

Apollo put his arm around me, feigning energy I knew he didn't have. "Alright!"

We needed as many willing participants as possible for this to work, so we were splitting up. Apollo would prepare things in this world while we worked the other.

Through the Friendly Society's bathroom closet, we returned to the Transpo Hub.

In a matter of hours, things had returned to normal. Time warped between worlds, so it was possible that days had passed. With the queen here, the attack on Mission Morality's HQ—the one we were trying to stop—would happen on her time.

Imprint sat cross-legged on the other side of the velvet ropes that demarcated the London closet queue. She looked bored, teleported away, and then blinked back in front of us, still bored. It wasn't until we'd all come through the closet door that she delivered a low-energy shrug, looking older and sadder than she should at her age.

"Hey." She stood. "You ready?"

"Actually, we've got a favor to ask," Brun-Brun said.

"Where's Enyo?"

"She... stayed back. We need your help."

"One sec," she said and teleported away, returning with a sandwich in hand. "Sorry, didn't want to lose that one."

"Can't buy a sandwich in the blink of an eye. Little young for stealin'," Benj scolded.

Brun-Brun glared at him and then turned to Imprint. "It's amazing. Can you explain your Spectrum ability?"

"I travel between places I've been to in the past two hours. This is Brunhilda's Butternut." She took a bite of the stolen sandwich. "They're the enemy, right? At least according to Enyo."

Benj tried to respond, but Brun-Brun shut him down with a preemptive glance. "And how long have you had a Brunhilda's marker?"

"I don't know," she answered. "Maybe a month? I hit snooze about a month ago and lost everything."

"Wow," Shǎng interrupted. "You sleep for less than two hours at a time!"

"That or reset all my markers. I hardly wake up anyway. I can usually fall straight back asleep, but yeah. Not all it's cracked up to be. What happened to Enyo? Why would she stay back?"

"She got hurt. She's recovering," Brun-Brun said.

"Really?" The way she said it seemed almost excited.

"She won't be coming back for a while."

A smile cracked on her face. "Thank God. I'm outta here. See ya."

"Wait!" Brun-Brun grabbed her, tethering himself to her ability, should she teleport away. "We need your help."

"I've been helping for years."

"One more. Please. The queen is targeting Mission Morality in the Arabian Desert. We need your help getting there."

"Queen's doing this. Queen's doing that. That's all Enyo ever said too."

"Why did you help her, then?"

"Didn't always want to, but I owed her. Ran to the street after the orphanage didn't work out. That's where she found me, right as I was—"

"Let me stop you there," I said. "Clearly there's a lot to unpack, but you seem like a straight shooter. I'm sorry about Enyo. She's a pain in everyone's ass, and I'm sure life's been tough. But today, I can only care about one thing—not two half things. You've repaid whatever debt you think you owe. The queen almost killed Enyo, if that makes you feel better. You're free. Do whatever you want after this. Two-hour teleport the world! But we need your help to make sure there's a world worth traveling to. Please?"

My friends recoiled at my insensitivity, but Imprint didn't teleport away.

"One," she said. "What do you need?"

Brun-Brun took over. "Rabin Square in Tel Aviv. That's where we'll meet you. We need you to take us to the Rub' al Khali in the Arabian Desert. Renegayd's attacking Mission Morality HQ, and when it happens, we need you to drop us right between them."

"I take people to places I've been before. How am I supposed to get to some random spot in the desert?"

"A man named Apollo is waiting on the other side of this door. He'll make sure you get markers in Tel Aviv and the desert. We'll meet you in Rabin Square. Then, you take us to the desert."

"That's it?"

"That's it," Brun-Brun said.

"Maybe you could get us back out too," Shǎng tried.

"It's more than one thing," Imprint said. "But fine. I'll help. Never been to the desert. Probably because it sounds horrible. Whatever."

"Great! Off you go!"

Brun-Brun practically shoved Imprint through the London closet door, and half the plan disappeared into Apollo's hands. Somehow he needed to get Imprint three thousand miles from London to Rub' al Khali. She needed a marker there to facilitate our interruption of the queen's attack. His lack of immediate plan was offset by his confidence that the Global Rights Organization would get the job done. Everything hinged on his ability to get Imprint to the desert—and our ability to recruit Empaths.

"Couldn't we have asked her to take us back to Enyo's compound before chucking her back to London?" Shǎng asked.

"Sam was pushin' our luck already." Benj slapped me on the back, beaming.

"Ow! I'm fragile!" I laughed. "We don't have time for another sob story. I'm sure Enyo manipulated her. We don't need to baby her."

"Not what I would have done," Brun-Brun said. "But it worked. Let's get going."

The open field between the forest and the city was peaceful compared to when we'd sprinted through it. Things had happened fast for a long time, but storming the Transpo Hub, visiting London… it felt surreal.

The secret underground passage wasn't quite as hidden as when we'd left it, thanks to a group standing guard at its entrance.

"Hey!" Benj shouted, recognizing the group as part of our army.

"They're angry," Shǎng warned.

Behind us, the trees shuddered as an invisible field dissipated to reveal the rest of our army blocking the path back to the field.

"Got 'em!" someone yelled, and the group standing guard surrounded us.

"Hey everyone," Adele said. "Thanks for the welcome wagon."

A woman with shock-white hair spit on the ground between us.

"Where were you?" she asked.

"You lied to us!" someone shouted from behind her.

"We had to get to London," I tried to explain. "Enyo wanted you to believe you were attacking."

"Believe we were attacking?"

"It's complicated. Look, we allied with the Global Rights Organization. We've got a plan, but we couldn't risk the queen spoiling things by reading your mind. I—"

"More deception!" Someone shouted behind me, and the circle of angry soldiers tightened around us. "More lies!"

"I'll transmit the memory," Shǎng said. "If you're an Empath, don't block me."

Before anyone could protest, he placed his fingertips to his temple, and the ground dropped away. We flew through the forest canopy into the sky. Someone screamed, but it echoed away as we dropped into his memory of G-A-Y. In rapid speed, Shǎng showed the meeting with the Global Rights Organization—all of it—up until standing in the forest receiving Shǎng's memories.

"No more lies," he transmitted before setting us back into reality and continuing verbally. "We need your help. We don't have time for secret plans. We have to work together."

Brun-Brun explained the plan we'd all seen. "Renegayd is going to attack Mission Morality's fortress. The queen intends to kill them."

A few people chuckled, and one said, "We'd be happy watching them exterminate each other."

"I know they've hurt us," Brun-Brun said. "But they aren't the enemy. The enemy is the hate on every side of this war. Renegayd, Mission Morality, *us*... we're all feeding it, and until we stop there will always be more. It's *hate* that's keeping us from equality."

Shǎng grabbed Benj's hand and stepped toe to toe with the angry circle. "You want to see the queen die? Go join Mission Morality. You want to kill Mission Morality? Then join Renegayd. We have work to do."

Brushing shoulders, Shǎng led Benj through the group and slipped out of the circle. Adele followed, then Brun-Brun.

"We have to try something new," I said before following after.

At the cusp of failing before even beginning, we regained our army. There wasn't much time; so, recruitment had to be aggressive. We needed Empaths, but we'd take anyone. Our army was to sneak into the city and contact anyone who might be willing to help. If they agreed, they were instructed to meet us at Transpo Hub Square after Renegayd left the city. Our resistance would grow by however many recruits showed up, and we'd all take the Tel Aviv closet door to meet Imprint.

Empaths were the exception to widespread recruitment. They were to be approached with extreme caution. We couldn't afford to share our plan with Empaths who might not join us. Any failed recruitment attempt risked exposing everything. We couldn't hide, but it was still meant to be quiet—as quiet as a small army recruiting from a larger one could manage.

Benj, Shǎng, Adele, and I stuck together, contacting all our friends except the Scales of Justice. The Ivory Tower was off limits, and we weren't willing to gamble a trip in *her* elevator to get to their meeting place.

Each day I expected to hear something had gone wrong, but we snuck in and out of the city without conflict. I couldn't accept that we were evading detection. It seemed the queen didn't want to interfere. Net yet.

Chapter 23

Fruits of Recruitment

"Shouldn't we use our own name?" Benj stretched across the table, reaching for the Orgie.

"What do you mean?" Shǎng passed him the bottle.

"Can't we call it somethin' besides *the queen's attack*? At least pretend it's our thing, instead of reactin' to hers?"

"Night before our intervention?" Shǎng laughed. "Ooh! Night before our desert vacay!"

Benj howled, and Brun-Brun snatched the Orgie off the table.

"Is this a good idea?" Brun-Brun asked.

"No hangovers," Shǎng said. "We're restless, B. Come on."

Benj leaned over and snatched the bottle back. He passed it to Shǎng, who pecked his cheek.

"Could do you some good."

"I'll pass," I said.

"Wonder how many will meet us," Shǎng said.

Nobody responded. It wasn't worth guessing. We'd show up at the Transpo Hub and transport through the Tel Aviv door alone if we had too.

Brun-Brun stood up. "I'm calling it a night. Tomorrow will be here soon, and I like old-fashioned rest."

Shǎng and Benj were rubbing noses, and Adele rolled her eyes.

"Am I gonna have to push you out your chair?" She pointed at the hall to Brun-Brun's departing back. "Don't make me come over there."

If there were ever a time to make things right, this was it. There might not be another chance. We hadn't really talked since London, but avoidance didn't mean we'd resolved it.

"Wait up!" I shouted, jogging to meet Brun-Brun. "Can we talk?"

"What's up?" he said, not slowing his pace.

"Ha. A lot."

"Yeah."

I let my hand find his, and when they touched he stopped.

"I miss you," I said. "I still feel bad."

"I've been thinking about it. Obviously," he added, meaning to be funny. "I can *see* why you did it, but I can't understand it."

"I'm sure Apollo would say that's called being human. But for what it's worth, I'm sorry."

"None of it matters," he said. "Can't expect you to murder the Queen of Witches days after arriving. So it was all going to happen anyway."

My guilt bubbled to the surface. "Even if I'd known this would happen, I don't know if I'd have killed her. I know how that sounds, like I'm more comfortable orchestrating death, but it's not me."

That was way more serious than I'd intended for this conversation.

"We're all consenting to death every day." Brun-Brun continued down the hall. "Only way to stop it is to kill yourself, and that's what we're trying to stop."

"That's kind of a fucked-up thought," I said.

"I think I was scared by how bad you could hurt me. Geez, how stupid to let a stranger affect me like that. We barely knew each other, and I was furious!"

"I was being infuriating," I said.

"It shouldn't have mattered… but it did."

I rested my hand on his arm when we reached his door. "I cared too much too."

"So what, then?" he asked. "Enjoy our last night?"

"Caring too much for someone. That's something more, Brun-Brun. I'm sorry about everything, but despite all this shit, I fell in love with you."

He seemed shocked.

"I—"

He didn't know what to say. I'd messed it up again, but this time I felt vulnerable, like he could shatter me with the wrong words or with nothing at all.

He reached behind him and turned the handle. "I love you too."

We crashed into each other, my head knocking his chin.

"Oh! Fu—! Ha!" He laughed, checking his lip for blood.

We kissed, fitting together this time as we closed ourselves off from the world into his room. He took my shirt off first, kissing my neck when it was shed. His skin was warm, his stubble rough, and his breath trembled.

When he took his shirt off, his wings shuddered, flexing out from his profile. I rushed to hold him, scared he might fly away before I'd get the chance.

He reached for my jeans, and I unzipped his. It was different from that first day in the Ivory Tower. We were careful with each other, taking turns, sharing control, laughing, kissing, loving. With little more knowledge of each other than our first meeting, affection guided us. We'd both transformed, shaving jagged corners and rough edges to fit.

I wanted time to know him.

So, we took it slow, exploring each other. Passionate sprints joined gentle nothings, and with every minute my adoration deepened. The morning came long before I was ready, and then we were the two having an Orgie at breakdfast.

"Uh-huh," Shǎng teased. "Who's irresponsible again?"

Word came that Renegayd had gone through the portal, and our timer started. We were many, but not enough to stop an army—let alone two. With any luck, the recruits joining at the Transpo Hub would triple or quadruple our numbers. If no one was there, we'd lose. If Apollo couldn't get Imprint to the desert, we'd lose. And even then, our plan had never been tested. There was a chance that no matter what we did, we'd lose.

We led the group through the field to the edge of town. The city was empty, but I felt my still Blank Canvas manifest in vulnerability. Brun-Brun must have felt it too, because he stayed glued to my side.

Shǎng stopped us before the turn into Transpo Hub Square. "Wait for our signal," Shǎng communicated.

We turned the corner and my heart sank. Six people waited by the bronze statue on the hill. Six recruits was far less than I'd hoped, but as they approached I realized it was worse than that. I should have known. The Scales of Justice always stayed behind.

"Hello there!" Jacob called, spotting us before we could duck back around the corner. "This must be Dream Boy. Wow. Worth all this?"

"Hey Jacob," I said, feeling awkward and estranged from my old San Francisco friend. "Guess you've got your Spectrum ability?"

He turned to the side, and a black tail whipped through the air. His goofy smile hadn't changed.

"Congrats."

"Hey Lou," I greeted the other person I recognized. "And you all must be the new Scales members?"

"What are you doing Sam?" Lou said. "We're after the same thing. Adele, Renegayd is trying to bring an end to hate."

Adele tried to reason with her. "You're not ending it. You're reflecting it back. Can't you see that attacking Mission Morality is more of the same?"

"I heard you've been telling people that." Jacob gestured to the empty square, "So where are they? Where's this mighty army that thinks destroying Mission Morality is so wrong?"

"Oh we're here," someone said, and an invisible field lifted, revealing hundreds of recruits crowding the square, edging the path that had allowed us to approach the Scales through the crowd.

"Jacob, join us!" I pleaded. "We can show the queen that change is possible without violence. We have a plan."

"I don't want to hear your plan! Renegayd sparked all of this! The reason any of this is happening is because *we* refused to back down. We're so close, and you're checking out because things got hard. I can't abandon people who need us because a few assholes might die along the way. If we have to eliminate every homophobic bastard to reach equality—we'll do it."

"Listen to yourself! This is crazy!"

"This is Renegayd!" Jacob cheered, backing off the hill as our recruits circled around us. "This is what we've worked for the whole time."

"You're wrong," I said. "Things changed."

"What changed? We're still getting bullied. We're still getting beaten!" His voice shook. "You're turning your back on us. It's you that changed, Sam. The cause is the same."

"But there's another way!" My throat tightened, and I fought back tears.

Shǎng instructed our army to file in after us into the already crowded square.

"Don't rehash things we've already covered, remember?" Jacob said, stepping back as our army overwhelmed them. "You want to slow things down. I can't accept someone who's seen what that means—the harm that causes—and still chooses to sacrifice those people."

"I know," I croaked, seeing our irreparability. "I'm sorry, but I understand."

"Fuck you," Jacob said as a tear fell down his cheek. "Come on."

He and the other Scales members ran up Main Street back to the tower, and my friends celebrated while I explored an old void that now felt permanent.

"We did it." Adele fist bumped our recruits. "Thank you for coming! Thank you!"

"Hya hya!" Benj hoisted Shǎng onto his shoulder.

"I'm sorry," Brun-Brun squeezed my hand before addressing the crowd. "Everyone, get through the Tel Aviv closet. Renegayd's already on the move."

The horde of resistance turned to enter the Transpo Hub, and we ran with the stream toward the purple door, where a long line of people formed, waiting to make the jump, single file, into Tel Aviv.

On the other side, people gathered to see our impromptu march. We linked arms—some even cheered. The mile walk from Shpagat's closet to Rabin Square felt powerful, a spontaneous parade. This was not a celebration, though. This was a march to battle. These were necessary steps to reach equality.

"Look!" Brun-Brun pointed in front of us. "City hall. We made it."

"Let's hope Imprint did too."

With so many behind us, we tried to stay confident entering the square, but it wasn't until Imprint casually nodded from the Yitzhak Rabin memorial that I took a real breath.

Apollo stood next to her.

"Holy shit. It's working," Adele said.

Brun-Brun hugged Apollo, who was beaming, and the relief that each side of the closet door had been successful spurred energy.

"You did it," Apollo said.

"Hard to know what we'll need," Brun-Brun said, "but it's a good turnout. Ready Imprint?"

"You're gonna want to leave soon," Imprint said, her perpetual boredom oozing. "Things are heating up out there."

I turned around, trying to soak up the scene but unable to see past the masses surrounding us. This could work. It had to work.

"Let's do it," I said.

In an unnatural blink we were no longer in Tel Aviv. Rabin Square became a scorched desert; our army stood in the blazing heat of the Arabian Desert, and in the open sea of sand it was easy to spot the monstrous fortress. Imprint had done it, landing us between Mission Morality's HQ and the massive Renegayd army.

We hadn't been the only ones recruiting.

Our resistance had filled Rabin Square, but here in the Rub' al Khali, we were a few more grains of sand between two powerful forces, the chokepoint of an hourglass that hadn't yet been turned. Shouting from both sides greeted our appearance.

Above the commotion boomed a voice that seemed to come from the sky.

Chapter 24

The Birth of Tragedy

"Hello, Mission Morality!" The queen sounded like she was hosting a party at the Ivory Tower. "Renegayd's just delighted to be here."

That roused laughter from her side, and Brun-Brun's hand met mine in uneasiness. We knew the queen could end this any time she chose.

"And of course let me not forget the bizarre third wheel standin' between us. Gimme a *heyy*!"

Our group responded with nervous silence and shifting weight.

"Huh," she said, her levity dissipating. "Mission Morality, I want y'all to remember that you chose this. You claim to embody the world's hatred for the LGBT community even though I made it clear we'd achieve Perfect Equality. You know ya can't win, and still you're standin' there, guns pointed at us, clinging to hate."

More silence, save a few shouts from Mission Morality, punctuated her presentation.

"Hate's a funny thing," she continued. "The stronger it is, the better it protects, and the more it exposes. Everything's out to get you when self-defense creates such a big opening, and like all—orifices—you just don't know how deep it goes until you poke around. Look, I hate bad hair days, but I'm not about to shave it all off. Let's see how deep your hatred runs."

The queen cackled, and a commotion from within Mission Morality's fortress spread across the desert. I reeled between the two armies, scanning for a sign of what happened. Mission Morality's fortress stirred. Bright flashes glinted across their fortress walls. Not flashes, but the sun reflecting off polished objects that had appeared from nowhere.

Shǎng explained what I couldn't make out from our distance. "She changed their weapons. Turned their guns into swords."

The queen's booming voice returned. "Sure you'll twitch your finger to shoot us, but what about up close? Would you rip hatred through us? Does your hate run deep enough to get… intimate? This is your chance. Charge out that fortress, cross the desert, and stick us with your swords. You know how the gays like to be impaled."

This was her plan. It had the Scales of Justice watermark. By forcing more action than a trigger pull, the chalkboard equation ensured only the most "helpful" eliminations. Some would stay back. The queen was baiting the real enemy, the ones between Renegayd and Perfect Equality.

"Come out, come out. We aren't contagious," the queen boomed. "But then, even spaghetti's straight, until it gets all hot and sweaty."

A rumble grew from the fortress until Mission Morality rallied a roar so loud it overcame the queen. The fortress became an anthill as Mission Morality scurried off the walls, pouring out of its open mouth to stand in front of their stronghold.

"She's taunting them," Apollo said.

Terror spread across our resistance as things drifted far from what we'd imagined. Resisting now meant being trapped between opposing forces that would collide *through* our meager line.

"Empaths! Get ready!" Brun-Brun shouted.

There were ten important members to our team: the Empaths who would invade the minds of both armies. By sharing memories across the battlefield, we hoped that Mission Morality could understand Renegayd and vice versa. It was too easy to hate some*thing* when it was not some*one*. Demonizing, dehumanizing, that's how wars are fought, but *re*humanizing might be how they're stopped. If opposing sides could understand each other, how could they fight?

The queen had armed Renegayd with swords too, transporting us back to a time when victories were determined by willpower instead of firepower. Still, the queen was a nuclear bomb, and I didn't expect her to fight fair.

"CHARGE!"

The queen lifted her wand, and a geyser of glitter spat into the desert air. By the time the first specks hit the ground the gap between the two armies had closed. There wasn't much time before we'd be trampled.

"Do it!" I shouted.

Our ten Empaths were spread across our resistance. We stood

side by side, facing alternate armies, each person holding the hand of the person next to them. This had to work; our thin line was useless if it came to forcing the waves from colliding.

The outreach began, and I scanned for signs it was working.

One skinhead charged straight for us, teeth gritted, eyes wide—the embodiment of hate—charging to kill Mission Morality. The man stumbled, overcome by the Renegayd throngs behind him, but not before I saw him grab his head, dazed by the flood of emotion we'd sent. I spun around to scan Mission Morality's approaching army, but Apollo confirmed as I witnessed for myself.

"It's working!"

One by one, the stampeding armies lost their front lines to the human comprehension we'd exchanged between them. Mission Morality received memories from Renegayd and from our resistance—the experience of being hated, the pain of it, the triumph of overcoming it, the joy and suffering of an entire life. Not Perfect Equality—but Perfect Empathy—and our Empaths shared from both sides. Lifetimes exchanged in an instant.

"There's too many!"

The armies were still approaching. Every soldier we stopped seemed to be replaced by two more.

"Keep going!"

Our resistance squirmed, uncertainty growing as the hordes approached. Brun-Brun found my scrambling gaze.

"We have to retreat," he said. "The queen was right. There's too much hate. We'll try something else, but we have to leave now. Imprint!"

He hugged me as Imprint removed our resistance in small

groups. Whoever was touching when she blinked back and forth was transported back to Tel Aviv. With twenty yards between either side, it was clear that there were no longer two sides. Wearing a rainbow vest or not, there was hate. We were infected—they were infected. Hate won.

Without us, there was no longer even a speed bump to slow hate from doing what it was made to do, ruin lives. Imprint appeared next to Brun-Brun and I. It was our turn, the last remnants of an inadequate attempt. Brun-Brun still hugging me, I saw the space between the two armies close.

A soccer mom lifted a broadsword over her head.

"Okay," I said, waiting for Imprint to make it disappear.

It didn't. The sword stayed skyward, and I wrenched my gaze from the woman to see both armies in a frozen portrait of combat. Sand blew beneath unmoving feet. It could only be one person, and I wriggled out of Brun-Brun's petrified embrace to address the queen.

"Pulling out?" she asked. "You know, I wanted to flick my wand. Your Scales of Justice thought this would tilt things utility positive. Yuck," she scrunched her forehead looking at the tip of a Renegayd dagger slicing someone's throat. "I can destroy Mission Morality."

"And start the next wave of hate with one fell swoop," I said.

She grumbled. "We'll stomp out hate. Wherever it is."

"I wasn't talking about you creating the next Mission Morality. I'm talking about Renegayd taking its place."

Her gaze was piercing. "You don't believe that."

"I can't understand why people hate gays… but I can see why they hate Renegayd."

"Well, la-dee-da. Hasn't time away from my tower made you snobbish?"

"This is not a simple problem, but you keep looking for a simple answer. Set up the equation and make sure it lands in your favor. Kill a thousand to save a thousand and one. There is a correct perspective on gay rights, but it's the same perspective everyone deserves."

"That's what we're fighting for!" she said. "Everyone who will live happily ever after because of us."

"How can the remainder be worth saving when the other variables are necessary sacrifices?"

"You tell me!" she said. "You argued the opposite."

"I was wrong."

"So what?!" She stomped her foot. "What would you do? Tell me what good you're doing other than obstructing hate's view of us?"

"Perfect Empathy. Our Empaths are sharing lives across the battlefield. We'll show Mission Morality that Renegayd is full of *people* and show Renegayd the same."

The queen sneered. "You've got too much faith in humanity."

"It was working. Everyone's present comes from their past. We're just products of our experiences. You should understand that. I can't even tell the difference between Renegayd and Mission Morality anymore."

"Oh please."

The queen slid her finger down a Renegayd soldier's sword. She yanked the sword from the woman's hand and placed the woman's palm on the Mission Morality stomach she'd otherwise have ripped open. She moved to the next Renegayd and pried away his sword before placing his empty hands on the shoulders of a disarmed Mission Morality soldier within arm's reach.

"What are you doing?" I asked.

She subdued the next Renegayd and repositioned one hand to cradle the frozen face of a Mission Morality.

"You know," the queen said, "all those people who've been telling you I'm a Blank Canvas were wrong. You're the only Blank Canvas. There is always one."

"Stop saying that," I said. "That doesn't mean anything."

"I used to be a Blank Canvas. Now, I'm the Artist. Brushing, pulling, scraping to progress, but you," her eyes flared, "you're my true masterpiece. I sure hope you learned something, because you were a pain in my ass."

"What are you talking about?"

"Hate can't be destroyed with a flash of empathy." She raised her eyebrows. "Revolution ain't for the sweet, Baby. It's an act of violence."

The queen took her wand from the purple fabric belt tied around her waist and swirled the air with it. She disappeared, replaced by a blur that transported around the battlefield, leaving a chain of disarmed soldiers touching some part of the opposite army. In no time, she'd reconfigured the battlefield, entangling the two armies by connecting opposites into thousands of mixed pairs.

"Got a few touchin' the naughty bits," she said, reappearing in front of the soccer mom, who still held her broadsword.

"What are you doing?" I asked again. "What is all of this for?"

Her heels clicked on the path she materialized as she walked toward me. After placing one of Brun-Brun's hands in mine, she extended her arm in a familiar way.

"You coming?" she said. I remembered doing this before—trusting, being let down—and yet I reached for her hand. "Empathy needs sacrifice."

She took a deliberate step in front of the woman's sword.

Our hands joined at the same time the sword pierced her heart, and time snapped back to life with a thunderous noise before it cut out. Not frozen, vanished. It was a second and a lifetime—played before me, with me, and through me.

*****

"Tell me this isn't true."

"What did we do?"

"This is not our daughter!"

The queen hid around the living room corner as his older sister came out of the closet. Before Dionysia, there was Dennis, and as his parents' shouting turned to sobbing he felt more pride in his older sister than he ever imagined. Enyo kept her chin high while they cried, and he couldn't quite place why he felt such a strong connection to his sister in that moment. Dennis knew he was different, but how so wasn't yet clear. The only thing clear that night was that his sister Enyo was the bravest and best big sister he could hope for.

Enyo started coming home with bruises. She was picked on at school, and then punished for acting up. She became cold, angry, and distant, but by pushing her parents away, she drove them closer to Dennis, their love manifest in packages and perks—baseball camps, monster trucks, dinosaurs, and Nerf guns. With each unboxed toy, Dennis noticed his sister's disgust, arms crossed, resolved not to care. His parents' love came at her expense. He didn't want toys; he wanted his big sister to know he loved her, and one day he flushed a G.I. Joe down the toilet in an act of solidarity.

"Mom!" Enyo smiled, ruffling his hair. "Better call a plumber!"

He was proud even if she enjoyed the flooding more than his sacrifice. He'd wanted an Easy-Bake oven anyway. As Dennis got older, two things became clear: that his parents were clinging to their *normal* son; and that he was not their *normal* son.

He was a prisoner.

His sister's freshmen year of high school was his first in middle school, the year he needed her most and the year she was farthest away. His brave lesbian sister was replaced by an empty room, and though he'd run to her crying, she'd slam the door shut cursing, the smell of pot leaking into the hallway.

She might not have seen the tears, or the eye shadow.

Enyo wasn't there for Dennis, and his parents were there only for Dennis. Alone, he attempted to help the girl trapped inside while everyone else reinforced her prison with simple, daily acts.

As Enyo's skin thickened, Dennis felt his nerves excavated, self-confidence brushed away until each pain receptor sat on the surface. His every action became a production. Dennis struggled to make eye contact, to convince even his own reflection that he was looking at someone, instead of out from someone. Why was he so exhausted by living?

Enyo found friends, the Munch Bunch, and they came to the house to demonstrate how loud, and fun, and full of life they were. Her happiness made things worse.

In eighth grade, Dennis fell asleep holding a bottle of Tylenol PM. He hadn't taken any, just cried himself to sleep thinking about it, unsure what would happen if he did.

Two shoeboxes hidden in the corner of his closet were his greatest relief. A pair of green stilettos he'd found on the street; a worn tube of crimson lipstick from his mom's purse; a gold necklace he'd stolen from Target; and a sequined dress nearly his size that he'd found lying on a bench outside school. He'd thought his heart might explode when he finally worked up the courage to unzip his bag and stuff the dress into it, but it was the best thing he'd ever done.

Now, in the privacy of his room, he could spin. Dizziness was a key part of the trick to leaving his own life to enter another. The night before his freshmen year of high school, he'd finished his routine of prayer and self-loathing to stand somehow courageous.

"I will love high school," he said to himself. "Somehow, I'll find something. Find people who like me. I will love high school."

The sound of his mom crying woke him, and he crept down the stairs, wondering what had happened to some neighbor or family member or president. It must have been bad, because his sister sat between both their parents on the couch. It was the first time he'd seen Enyo between them in a long time, and he smiled.

"Everything okay?" he asked.

"What the fuck is this?!" his dad screamed, kicking the coffee table, launching his worst nightmare—a shoebox—into the air.

His gold necklace scratched his face as it flew across the room. Enyo held out her cell phone, showing a photo she'd taken from his doorway. He collapsed. He couldn't breathe. Enyo's photo revealed him as her—arms spread wide, spinning under his ceiling fan, made even more horrible by the smile painted on his face.

"Get out."

"Dad!" He hated how his voice sounded sad, desperate, gay.

No! Get out of my house."

"Dad I—"

His dad wrenched the phone from Enyo and threw it against the wall. Everyone flinched, but Dennis broke. Wailing he apologized.

"Mom, please! Enyo!" He wished his sister's arms would unfold, that she'd unglue from the couch to save him. Say anything! A flash of anger swept over him. "This isn't fair. This is who I am!"

"That's not my son."

"I'm not your son!" Dennis said. "I'm not that person!"

"What. You're this? This... disgusting thing? Better gone. Better dead!" His dad hugged his mom. "You're breaking her heart! Get out of here!"

Dennis ran and missed his first day of high school wandering, not sure of anything. His phone vibrated:

Dad—don't bother coming home.

Dad—my son's already dead to me.

Dennis couldn't cry anymore. He was empty, broken. Then another message came:

Mom—I'm sorry. I love you. Dad is overreacting. We can fix this. We can get you help. It's not too late Dennis—we can fight it together. There are places that can help. People have gotten through this.

His finger quivered over the keyboard. He didn't want to respond. He didn't want to have these conversations, to go through these motions. Instead, he curled on a park bench, sweating and shivering until daybreak.

He feared home so much that school seemed like a haven. So he went, braving every hallway snicker tearing at his still-bleeding wound. But no one knew him at high school yet. He was invisible, and that gave him strength enough to make it to his locker.

High school was loud. A group of kids stood talking by his locker. Something felt off, but he clutched his backpack to his chest and tiptoed forward, creeping into dread wearing day-old clothes scarcely dry from sopping up tears. The kids weren't loitering; they were looking at his locker, pointing, laughing. He snuck through the crowd, avoiding eye contact until he was face-to-face with the image taped to the front of his locker: Enyo's photo.

Arms out, smiling, sequins shimmering in the 60-watt bulb of his room. As the group backed away from him, something he hadn't realized still remained broke: hope.

"Dennis? Dennis!" Someone called him, and his sister pushed through the group. She took in the scene before charging his locker to rip the picture off it. "What the fuck are you doing?" she shouted at the group.

"What are *you* doing?!" Dennis shouted back, voice cracking, to the delight of his audience.

"It wasn't me!" she answered. He recoiled, allergic to this stranger. "Jess must have texted it to herself!"

He hadn't heard her. None of it mattered. There was nothing

left. He'd been scared and sad, and it had come crashing down. Now there was only anger. Anger and Dionysia. Dennis was dead.

That day she found the portal and renounced her old world.

Years later, she discovered that one of Enyo's girlfriends had brought her sister there too. They were different people, but Dionysia avoided her. She'd forgiven the world, but not her. She wanted Enyo to find out she was alive when she became queen. *That would be revenge*, she thought. So she worked, and while she did, she watched the real world. Every runaway her reflection, every person an embodiment of her fantasy world. Here, everyone lived without judgment or anxiety.

That was what she wanted, and as she created it, the real world became unbearable in comparison. There was work, and power, and transformation… and then, there was Renegayd.

Chapter 25

Blank Canvas

Thinking back, it was at our moment of victory that I began yearning for what was irrevocably lost. In a transfer of heat, the queen's memory fell on me, as someone else's did for everyone there that day. A hurricane reshaped the world's landscape, a great shear supplanting erosional progress as hatred was replaced by sadness. Perfect Empathy—it turns out—is not a happy emotion. The queen's sacrifice was catalyst for the sharing she'd paired between Mission Morality and Renegayd.

The portals were well known, and though their use was still restricted to the LGBT community, each world lived in full awareness of its proximity to the other. People got used to the idea of an alternate universe filled with magic. It would become normal, unremarkable even, in no time.

Dramatic change forced people to adapt. Humanity would never have survived if we quibbled over enormities like alternate universes. Instead, we fight over things that don't matter, like what gender gets your neighbor hard.

Apollo helped steer the world toward normalizing gender and sexual identity. With Mission Morality and Renegayd linked, the two sides were equal halves to Perfect Empathy. Hatred had been dismantled, chopped and paired into stories of understanding between two people. Apollo organized these dyads for global enlightenment, teaching empathy through those who had already crossed the unfathomable divide.

It made sense that Apollo and the Global Rights Organization would lead the world to Perfect Equality. He used the queen's Perfect Empathy pairs, but history would remember the intervention in the desert as a victory of non-violence over violence. Only a few of us would debate it.

People say the Ivory Tower fell when the queen died, but the time shift between worlds makes it hard to know for sure. Her world seemed to *experience* life instead of just contain it. The city had to be built from the shadow and rubble of the old, but everyone here was used to rebuilding.

"I think she knew the whole time," said Benj, reaching across the table for the Orgie. "Knew exactly what she was doin'."

"You know, I could hand that to you," Shǎnguāng said, but Benj's mouth was already too stuffed to reply.

"She couldn't have predicted everything. She was smart. Saw an opportunity and took it," Adele said, looking to Brun-Brun. "Stole the whole idea from B and Apollo's Empathy plan anyway. Just did it bigger and better than we could."

Of course, I felt like I knew what happened. With needle and thread, Dionysia closed the divide across the battlefield: the queen shared her life with me, I shared mine with Brun-Brun, and so on. Apollo was right, in a way, because Empathy had generated the ultimate utility. The queen was also right. It took her power to change everything. With such a diverse group moved from hate to love, the first domino of human connection fell, starting a chain reaction that would surely lead to equality everywhere.

"Apollo's walking the path she paved for him," someone said.

"Apollo's a hero," I said. "No Spectrum abilities. A normal person doing the extraordinary."

"Come on, Sam," Shǎng teased. "What did *you* see? You were the one linked to the queen."

I took a drink of Orgie to cover up the refusal.

It wasn't the sequence of events that was secret. It was the queen's role in it, or at least the role she felt she played, that I wouldn't share. She wouldn't have wanted me to. I knew her, and though her glitter was a memory, it was so vivid I could hear her voice.

"Baby Cake Sweetie Pie," I imagined her saying, "You ready?"

Now that my canvas had been filled by everything she shared, it was my turn. I was no longer the Blank Canvas. She called it being the Artist, but artists didn't have power like this. It was more like being the Guardian, a warrior responsible for protecting love, for beating hate. Surrounded by my friends at the dinner table for the last time, I smiled. I didn't agree with the path she'd taken to get us here, but I couldn't deny the results. I would be lucky to get the same. *Revolution ain't for the sweet.*

That night Brun-Brun and I made love, the same as we had every night since that day in the desert. It was electric; it was perfect—of course—because he had been linked to me. He learned what I liked, what I didn't, and why.

I lay in bed, filled with anxiety, while he slept peacefully next to me.

As quiet as I could be, I unpeeled the covers and swung my feet out over the edge. Tiptoeing across the room, I found the bag I'd packed earlier and slung it over my shoulder. It wasn't until I was at the door that Brun-Brun spoke up.

"So this is it?" he said, and my heart, which had barely held on, dropped straight to the floor. He got out of bed to cradle me as I wept. "Shh shh."

"I'm sorry," I managed. "I can't stay."

"But it's over. We won!"

I hugged him, realizing that heartbreak was unavoidable. "This wasn't my victory. It was my preparation. Perfect Equality for LGBT people is just a step. We're still judging our reflection. There's still hate."

The moonlight came in from the window as he held my face in his tear-filled gaze. I kissed him. There was so much more to say: that I loved him, that he loved me. But we didn't say any of it. He knew everything I would have said and could have never said anyway. He knew me as well as I knew Dionysia. Knowing I wasn't strong enough, he did the hard part by turning away to climb back into bed.

I stepped out, into the streets and beyond the life of her city. The northern edge was abrupt. Main Street ended at green grass blowing in the night winds as far as I could see. Walking toward the world beyond, I wondered if she had left this part untouched on purpose. For me.

"Sam?" The voice stirred emotions I'd never felt before.

"Enyo." I turned to find the queen's big sister standing at the end of Main Street. Her throat had healed, but the scar would never disappear completely.

"You were linked with him, weren't you?" I didn't say anything, just felt new feelings. "I have to apologize. I shouldn't have shown anyone the photo. I shouldn't have even taken it! I should have helped. I was jealous, and then I realized he wasn't perfect, and…."

Why would she come here? Why would she talk to me? The queen didn't want to deal with her. That's why she let her hide in the Ivory Tower; that's why she let her live. Enyo looked hollowed by memories she could never put to rest, still refusing to recognize her own hate. My rage surprised me. Fists balled, I considered letting it go, but couldn't bring myself to leave.

"Your brother's been gone for decades," I said. "Now, your sister's dead, and you want to apologize for a photograph? *I* can't forgive you!"

"I feel terrible!"

"It was never about how you felt! You were her hero! You outed her, and then refused to accept who she was."

"But… I'm sorry. Dennis never understood that."

"Her name was Dionysia."

The complicated spell was easy. Enyo fell to the ground. Her heart stopped, body sprawled on the city street, hands reaching for the grass beneath my feet. I left her there and headed north. With my first real decision as Guardian, I could do the queen this favor. Sometimes, eliminating hate is Utility Positive.